THE
TYRANNY
OF FLIES

HarperVia

An Imprint of HarperCollinsPublishers

THE TYRANNY OF FLIES

A NOVEL

ELAINE VILAR MADRUGA

TRANSLATED BY KEVIN GERRY DUNN

HarperCollins books may be purchased for educational, business, or sales promotional use. For information, please email the Special Markets Department at SPsales@harpercollins.com.

Originally published as *La tiranía de las moscas* in Spain in 2021 by Editorial Barrett.

FIRST HARPERVIA EDITION PUBLISHED IN JUNE 2024

Designed by Janet Evans-Scanlon
Illustration © Alekss/stock.adobe.com

Library of Congress Cataloging-in-Publication Data has been applied for.

ISBN 978-0-06-333073-3

24 25 26 27 28 LBC 5 4 3 2 1

For Carlo, to the doors of my life.
And for Tía Cuca, in memoriam, with coffee and two gardenias.

ANGEL: In this house no one knows anything!
Where's my whip!

—Virgilio Piñera, *Cold Air*,
translated by Maria Irene Fornes

FOREWORD:
The Things You Just Can't Touch

I'm thirty-five years old. At times I'm struck by an overwhelming sense of adulthood and at others by the conviction that I am, in fact, an adult. These are two distinct phenomena: feeling is one thing and knowing is another. In this foreword to *The Tyranny of Flies* by Elaine Vilar Madruga (Havanna, Cuba, 1989), we're going to cite the philosopher Agustín García Calvo (Zamora, Spain, 1926–2012) extensively, because Vilar Madruga has written a novel that, perhaps accidentally, fictionalizes (and therefore amplifies) García Calvo's 1988 talk "How to Murder a Child to Make a Man (Or Woman)."[1] It is from this text that we have drawn the difference between feeling and knowing, a difference that we cannot and should not attempt to define, because to define something is to murder it. García Calvo came to things by groping around in the dark.

---

1   The original Spanish text of this talk, given on December 13, 1988, is available for free at www.editoriallucina.es. This foreword, however, quotes the version García Calvo gave on September 26, 1989, which can be accessed more easily at www.bauldetrompetillas.es. All English translations in this foreword are by Kevin Gerry Dunn.

. . . it seems that these not-dead things, well, they feel, they can feel. They're capable of feeling. Feeling is what they do. I can't explain the verb much better than that, because if I start trying to offer definitions, I run the risk of screwing everything up. This verb functions by dint of its own non-definition. They feel, they feel: it seems that feeling is what living things do, Calvo said on that December 13. He continued: *Feelings aren't something we know: if there's one thing we can say about feelings, it's that they are unknown, it's exactly what I was saying before about the verb "to feel": we can't touch it with a definition, its beauty is that we can't lock it up inside a definition. To know a feeling is to force it into a prison cell; and when you imprison a thing that consists precisely in remaining undefined, you murder it, obliterate it, make it disappear.*

Feeling is for the living. Knowing is for the dead. Feeling is inherent to childrenhood (that's not a typo, it's García Calvo). Knowing is inherent to adulthood. Childrenhood (which is most commonly found in children) is alive. Adults—you and me and most of our friends—are dead as fuck. What's happening to me, then, when after reading Vilar Madruga, García Calvo, or Alexanthropos Alexgaias (our next ally), I'm struck by that sense, or that knowledge, of my own adulthood? That's death itself—the apotheosis of State and Capital, also known as patriarchy or "structural authoritarianism, adultocentrism, and commercialism" (Alexgaias, 2013, p. 24)—and it's stalking me, pouncing on me, gobbling me up. Because I am, of course, the perfect prey: according to Alexgaias, I'm in the age bracket where my privileges are at their zenith. But the feeling of death isn't a genuine feeling at all, in the same way that, as García Calvo reminds us in his talk, a child who learns by rote to say he loves both Mommy and Daddy doesn't actually love either one. The feeling of death, like the knowledge of death, is a stage of assimilation into the Order (with a Garciacalvonian capital *O*), also known as assimilation into the prevailing system of adultocentric governance, as described in *The Antiadult Manifesto* by Alexanthropos Alexgaias (age seventeen) [the author includes their age in parentheses when signing their name].[2]

Vilar Madruga presents us with a fable that's dark, slick, and salacious (like a drama or a pussy) to illustrate these concerns, concerns that your typical adultist reader would write off as Peter Pan–ish or pretentious, or even as a fascioliberal attempt to vindicate youth by denigrating the elderly. The (nearly always adultocentric) literary-critic corps may well slap the stigmatizing label of "junior" or "didactic" on *The Tyranny of Flies*, given the publishing world's unabashedly adultocentric segregation of so-called children's literature (which is further segmented into the "YA" market) from what the canon considers capital-*L* Literature, which, as the platonic ideal, has no need for an ageist descriptor (though it is nevertheless stratified into dozens of other categories, starting with the current vogue for literature about/according to/against/before/behind/between/beyond/by/concerning/considering/for/from/into/of/on/regarding/through/under/with women).

But what a splendidly didactic novel Vilar Madruga has written, my friends! What an illustrious tradition of fabulism

---

2 Spanish text available for free at http://comunizar.com.ar/el-manifiesto-antiadultista.

The Tyranny of Flies has taken up! If only as a child I had gotten my hands on a book like this, a book that invites kids to rebel against their parents, and not in a metaphorical sense: Vilar Madruga gives us ample reason not to talk some sense into our parents, not to win them over for the common good, but to fucking murder them already, like the Orwell of *Animal Farm*! Strung on the same string of anti-adultist pearls as Salinger's *The Catcher in the Rye*, Saint-Exúpery's *The Little Prince*, Atxaga's *Memoirs of a Basque Cow*, Matute's *The Foolish Children*, and Obiols's *El tigre de Mary Plexiglàs* (the first book I read in Catalan, which, to my surprise, turned out to be a punk masterpiece regularly assigned in high schools), we find *The Tyranny of Flies* stewing in its own sinfulness. Starting with what García Calvo calls the sin of "a woman's hyperactive imagination":

> *Domination of women's imaginations is [. . .] one of the core functions of a patriarchal society's educational processes [. . .]. Indeed, it recognizes that an unfettered or hyperactive imagination in a woman is among the most radical threats to the patriarchal order, which is why society goes to great lengths to keep it in check.*

Think about the first sentence that the wardens of formal education wrote on the chalkboard and made us read out loud: *Mommy loves me*. And don't forget the first image they made us draw while confined within the walls of the preschool penitentiary: a portrait of our family. But in *The Tyranny of Flies*, Mommy doesn't love you and Daddy doesn't pose with you and your siblings under squiggly rays of sunshine. In *The*

Tyranny of Flies, your big sister is a Shakespearean heroine named Casandra locked in an epic struggle for sexual self-determination against the tyrannical reactionism of her father and the pathologizing reactionism of her mother.

> *Shakespeare*, Casandra writes on page 58, *understood all this way better than I do. Way better than anyone, really, because when Juliet appeared on her balcony, she didn't gaze at Romeo, no; she pressed her body against that chunk of carved rock, pressed her body against it to receive all its love and desire, the ardor of Veronese limestone, more eternal than the affections of any Romeo. With Elizabethan dramaturgy you have to read between the lines, okay? Just read Shakespeare between the lines and you'll see Juliet's passion for the objects of her affection. Don't take my word for it, my name is Casandra and I live in the heat of this endless summer's day, which is neither lovely nor temperate; listen to Shakespeare, he was a much better, prettier writer.*

Our protagonist and primary narrator has performed the finest possible exegesis of *Romeo and Juliet*. Fully Shakespearean but without a hint of romanticism (bearing in mind that Shakespeare was a total pussy, i.e., a drama queen, i.e., dark and slick and salacious, as I explained above), her hyperactive imagination is actually pure lucidity about aliveness and deadness, about sincere feeling and learned knowledge (the latter category includes romantic love, among other things): she's gripped by a genuine passion for objects, and her sweetheart of choice is a bridge, which Casandra rightly addresses using she/her pronouns ("I don't know which displeases Dad more," Casandra writes, "that I'm pining for a bridge, or that the object of my desire has a feminine essence"):

> *"It's a generalization that will facilitate both of us channeling this dialogue toward your erotic interest in objects . . . now tell me, are you not attracted to human beings?"*
> *"No."*
> *"Why is that?"*
> *"Another dumb fucking question."*
> *"Why is that?"*
> *"Humans don't smell like iron oxide."*
> *"That's a good point. Are you talking about your . . . affinity . . . ?"*
> *"The word is 'relationship.'"*
> *"A relationship is a bond between two people, Casandra. Something inanimate cannot offer any sort of bond."*
> *"According to you. What do you know? I've never seen anything more inanimate than Dad. And you still slept with him, didn't you?"*

The Tyranny of Flies describes the family and the State as two inherently violent structures, two great allies in sustaining oppression. The dialectical relationship between parents and children supports the dialectical relationship between the people and the State, and vice-versa. Given this book's Cuban origins, some occidocentric, omphaloskeptic readers will think that its criticism extends only to the Communist regime and not their own Capitalist democracies. Wake up, my ballot-clasping friends: Casandra, Calia, and Caleb's tyrannical father—a stutterer by grace of the Revolution and therefore a converter of all he touches into shit like a feculent King Midas (he calls his children Caca-sandra, Caca-lia, and Caca-leb)—is no different than your own congressmen and MPs when they drone on about how wee-wee the people must do our civic doo-doo-duty; about ho-ho-hope and cha-cha-change; about getting the president im-pee-pee-peached and getting Brexit duh-duh-done; even pretending they believe blah-blah-Black lives matter.

Cunning is the weapon of the enslaved. Like García Calvo, Vilar Madruga knows this, feels it, and puts it into practice in her work. Her collection of rabid short stories, *La hembra alfa* ("Alpha Female," published by Guantanamera in Seville in 2017 and regrettably unavailable in English translation), anticipates *The Tyranny of Flies* with characters whose ardor can withstand any humiliation. Locked in a dark room, confined to a wheelchair, and fully paralyzed except for the one hand she uses to masturbate, the protagonist of the story "El tercer círculo" ("The Third Circle") continues to pleasure her body even after being effectively blinded by her mother, who nails wood planks over the windows so the protagonist can no longer arouse herself by spying on the neighbor and his flaccid, leaky cock. To continue getting herself off, she uses her imagination and also her fingernails, which she bores into the wood for months until she has carved a crack through which she can indulge her prurient interests. And fuck, this woman's orgasms are enough to make the rest of us yearn for a tyrannical mother like hers. In another of the stories in the collection, the titular "Alpha Female" acquires the habits and strength of a lioness and takes to the streets on all fours, roaring a colossal "where the fuck are the males [. . .] this place is no grassland. No, not at all. Doesn't smell like mud or dry antelope shit, and even less like freedom. But even so I run, I run, I run among the sounds of the car horns."

What pleasure-seekers like most of all are the things you just can't touch with the lethal hand of definition. Like García Calvo and the mystic poets, Vilar Madruga knows this, feels it, and puts it into practice. That being the case, let's open *The Tyranny of Flies* with this feast of a song, which could very well have been written by St. Teresa of Ávila for the lute and tabret, but which was actually written by the Argentine band Intoxicados for drums, guitar, and electric bass:

The Things You Just Can't Touch

I like chasing women, I like marijuana,
And I like my guitar, James Brown, and Madonna
I like playing with puppies, I like playing my CDs
And I like parties in the street and hanging out and such
But what I like most of all
Are the things you just can't touch
I like going shopping on someone else's dime
And I like when friends come over just to kill some time
Yeah I like that light, and I like that shade
I like playing the bands that never get played
I like fast cars, but I like trains and boats too
I like when you're on time so I don't have to wait for you
Oh yeah I like rice, and I like puchero stew
I like red, green, yellow, and black, not so much blue
But what I like most of all
Are the things you just can't touch

That's why I like rock
Because rock, I don't touch it
I listen to it
Swallow it
Digest it
Swallow it again
(. . .)
But I better not say it
I don't wanna
I don't wanna
Because that just ain't rock
That ain't rock
That ain't rock
It ain't rock
It ain't rock
It ain't rock
That ain't rock
That ain't rock
(. . .)[3]

Cristina Morales
Rome, February 15, 2021
Translated by Kevin Gerry Dunn

3   Los Intoxicados, "Las cosas que no se tocan," *Otro día en el planeta Tierra*, Tocka Discos, Buenos Aires, 2005, CD.

CASANDRA

The flies talk to us, okay? This is fly country. Flies fly all around us, a nation of ideas buzzity buzz buzzing above Calia's head. She's unfazed, as usual, focused on her drawing of an elephant. The drawing, anatomically precise, isn't just the product of boredom and the summer heat. Calia never even looks up. One of the fattest flies lands on her forehead and wends its way over the pores and hairs and sweat droplets, flaps its wings, cleans them, what a lovely spot it's chosen to watch the action, to contemplate the elephant drawing, to admire and extemporize upon Calia's artistry and offer a thoughtful critique of her work. For example, the fly might remark that the elephant in the drawing is more than just a realist rendering of the original pachyderm, it might observe that the elephant is actually flawless, so perfect it's practically alive, and the fly might wonder if, any moment now, an invisible curtain will drop down Calia's sheet of paper, a closing flourish in the miraculous process by which the elephant draws breath and takes solid form. The fly dreams of landing atop the elephant's hulking gray mass. A beautiful mass. Notes of dung.

The fly waits on Calia's forehead.

An exercise in patience.

Do the flies dream of her drawings?

We do.

Just three years old. No, not the flies. The flies are much younger than my sister.

No one remembers when Calia started drawing. At this point, we just assume she was born with a paintbrush in hand and made her first watercolor with strokes of blood, amniotic fluid, and the mucus plug. I guess some anatomical masterpiece must've emerged from her experience in the birth canal; in any case, she never stopped, and the drawings keep multiplying like ants.

Her oeuvre can be studied, like any other genius's, according to her obsessions. Calia only draws animals. Like I said (and the flies are clearly also interested), her drawings aren't clumsy doodles like you'd expect from a kid her age, the page sinking under the weight of so much colored wax; they're fucking perfection. She started with insects. Ants were her favorite. And spiders. I'd say that was her darkest period. Drawings of predatory ants and spiders at the exact moment they dismembered their prey, a victim that was no longer animal but merely an object of the hunt, caught in a state of limbo between the jaws of death and the remote possibility of escape. Then came the birds. Mostly sparrows. It's easy to understand the rationale behind that pictorial decision. The only birds Calia has ever seen are the few emaciated sparrows that still fly in this country, fenced in by hunger and heat, sparrows with hearts as small as the pad of your little finger, sparrows that go into cardiac arrest and expire in people's gardens. After that, Calia moved on to monkeys. Monkeys with big fat asses. Veiny and bulbous, swaths of reds and purples. Those monkey butts brought an explosion of color to Calia's formerly sober pages.

And that brings us to today. Her elephant period. Thankfully, Calia hasn't yet considered what the genitals of an elephant in heat look like. She's just focused on their hooves, the shades of gray in their wrinkles and scars, the spindly hairs on their trunks.

To be clear, I have nothing against Calia's gift. I think it's great she spends so much time drawing—I just wish she was worse at it. That'd be a relief to everyone. It'd help us be more patient with the parade of monkey butts and spider legs. Couldn't she at least make the monkey butts and spider legs a little less lifelike? Or just draw a square house in front of mountains and a yellow sun, the typical awkward sketch kids are supposed to enjoy making and that everyone thinks is so adorable because it proves their baby girl has artistic inclinations? That'd be ideal.

Jesus, my stupid brain. I forgot to explain the most important thing, though you might've figured it out by now.

In case you haven't, my sister is three years old but she doesn't talk, okay? Or I mean, she doesn't want to talk. To us. She doesn't find the prospect enticing. Moving her mouth, inhaling air, and transforming it into words doesn't fall within the scope of Calia's interests, and Calia doesn't do anything she considers boring. In some ways, I admire my sister. She doesn't waste time. Not even with her family. Not even with the flies that keep landing, one after the other, on her forehead. Calia is patient, doesn't shoo them away. Calia is the ideal nation for the flies.

I left something else out. My stupid brain.

I left out the terror.

I'm gonna try and explain everything in an orderly manner, okay?

It's not just that Calia draws perfect animals, animals so lifelike you wonder why they don't step off the page; why they don't acquire length, width, and most important, depth; why the copulating monkeys remain forever frozen mid-thrust; why the sparrows are continually dying of strokes that explode their pinky-pad-size hearts; why the spiders are endlessly attacking their prey; and why the elephants never lift their trunks from the grass.

It's not just my sister's silence, her refusal to consider us more important or intellectually advanced than the flies. As far as Calia is concerned, we're all insects.

Though I guess that's a big part of the problem.

The terror has to do with our status, in Calia's eyes, as invisible creatures.

The terror has to do with her eyes.

Calia is our master. When she deigns to acknowledge us in any way, lifting her head to look at us, it's because *something* is happening.

Something very bad.

When Calia is not pleased, the external signs are immediate. She scratches an eyebrow, blinks once, slackens her jaw, stops sweating. The flies stop landing on her. Shit. The flies understand that the nation known as Calia has turned hostile. When you notice animals running away, you run too, okay? That's what everyone says and everyone is right. When the bugs stop buzzing, you stop talking. Shit, fuck, shit. The flies are onto something and Calia's mouth is moving, God help us if she says our names, God help us if she starts drawing butterflies, please, God, I'm sorry, she can draw whatever she wants, it's fine, she can keep doing elephants, she can keep doing monkey butts, those gorgeous, inflamed monkey butts, those glorious, hyperrealistic monkey butts, but not a butterfly, we all know a butterfly flapping on the page could be fatal.

If Calia draws a butterfly, we are definitively fucked.

Urban legend or family lore, I don't know and don't particularly care. We just know for sure that Calia is a ticking fucking time bomb.

Our family probably doesn't deserve to be saved. That's what Mom says in her best self-help-book voice, and she might not be wrong. We're not good people, okay? If we were, the flies would land anywhere except our bodies. And all of us—Mom, Dad, Caleb, Calia, and me—are always covered head to toe in flies. Dad says it's because we live in a hot country, that's how he consoles himself, but we all know it's bullshit. The flies feast on our sweat. Salty, sugary sweat, or rotting flesh, either one, doesn't matter; truth doesn't matter either.

Every family is different and freakish in its own way, but ours brought home the gold in the dysfunction Olympics.

You can tell because the flies go straight to Caleb. To die. They land on him, then fall to the ground, lifeless ink blots with withered wings. Caleb sweeps them up in his hand. It's what he does best. Animals are drawn to my brother. He makes them suicidal. Caleb is like an open grave. And he likes it. He loves being an open grave, the sick fuck. It gives him a purpose in life.

I was the first seed of evil. Or I mean, I'm the oldest. Sorry, I don't want my words to confuse you. I'll start over. Telling your own story in the first person is hard.

I wasn't always the big sister.

Before Caleb and Calia were born, it was just me, Casandra.

How old are you now, Casandra?"

"I told you, Mom, I'm seven."

"Remember what I told you: when we're in this space, I'm not your mother."

"Okay, Mom."

"I'm your therapist and I'm here to help with your neuroses. Does that make sense, Casandra? It's like a game, a super-duper fun game where we make believe I'm not your mother. Ready to play?"

"Okay, Mom."

"So, Casandra. You said you're seven years old. You look older. You're very tall for your age. Do you want to tell me why you've been feeling so sad lately?"

"I'm not sad."

"Are you sure?"

"Uh-huh."

"Well, I think you're mistaken. It might be a good time for some self-reflection. Are you sad, Casandra?"

"Dunno."

"Then why do you cry so much?"

"Camera broke."

"But that can't be everything. There's something else, you can't fool me. Let me see if I can guess . . . maybe you miss Dad? Have you been crying because your father isn't home very often? You have to understand, Casandra, you're a young woman now. Seven, right? You're old enough to know your father is a very important man."

"Mustache says so too."

"Who is this 'Mustache,' Casandra?"

"Pop-Pop Mustache. He lets me sit on his lap. Dad loves him lots."

"Casandra! Don't ever let me hear you say that again."

"Say what?"

"What you just said is very bad, Casandra. Very, very bad! And very dangerous! Your father could get in a lot of trouble if they found out you use that name to refer to—"

"To Pop-Pop Mustache?"

"—to Our Leader! Casandra, are you doing this on purpose?"

"No, Mom."

"I'm not your mother right now, I'm your therapist."

"Can you still punish me even though you're not my mom?"

"Listen to me. Look me in the eyes, Casandra. This is important. Swear to me you'll never say the words 'Pop-Pop Mustache' ever again."

"Okay."

"If anyone heard you saying that, they would take all your father's medals away. Christ knows what would happen to this family. The walls have ears, Casandra, don't you ever forget."

"I don't like Dad's medals. They're pokey."

"Well, do you want your dad to stop being such an important man to our country? Do you want your father to cry?"

"Dunno."

"Why don't you try doing some self-reflection, then answer me again."

"Crying's bad."

"Very bad! But that's exactly what will happen to your dad, and it will be your fault."

". . . but Pop-Pop Mustache loves me. He said so."

"Casandra!"

"Pop-Pop Mustache buys me dolls for my birthday."

"Well, if you want more dolls, do you know what you ought to call him?"

"Uh-uh."

"Leader."

"Leader Mustache!"

"Don't be smart with your mother, you little shit!"

"You're not my mother."

"Of course I'm your mother . . . and your therapist. Do you know what the consequence is for bad little girls like you, Casandra? They get reprimanded and punished . . . in times like these, your father has to work harder than ever before. He's earned his medals, but every single day, he has to prove he's faithful to Our Leader. If he doesn't, you won't get any more dolls. Do you understand?"

"Uh-huh."

"Then why are you crying?"

"Dad's camera broke!"

"Your father is an important man—he just needs the people who are even more important to remember that. It's very simple. Daddy is a hero, Casandra! Here, dry your face."

"I don't wanna."

"I said dry it. Do you want to keep telling me—"

"When something breaks, does it die?"

"I suppose. If it's irreparably broken, yes, sure."

"Dad said his camera's broken forever. Can you really break a person the same as you can break a camera?"

"Where did you hear that?"

"From Pop-Pop Mustache."

"Casandra! Again?"

"He says that at Dad's job, people come and go like ants and then they break."

"That's enough, Casandra. You can forget about all that. It's best not to pay attention when Our Leader says that sort of thing. Do you understand? It's best not to think about uncomfortable topics that don't concern you. Let's change the subject . . . I can't help you if you aren't honest with me. We're here to discuss you and not your father. Please stop projecting. Let's talk about Caleb for a minute. Do you love your brother?"

"It's his fault the bunny died."

"That rabbit was sick, it had cancer."

"It went to Caleb to die. It pricked up its ears and then that was it, it stopped hopping."

"Why don't you love your brother?"

"And the turtle, the turtle died too."

"That wasn't Caleb's fault."

"He just touched it, and it stopped poking its head out."

"The turtle was old, Casandra."

"I don't want to be near him. Everything goes to Caleb to die."

"You're a girl with a hyperactive imagination, Casandra, and that isn't a bad thing. To the contrary, it can even be beneficial.

But sometimes, if we use our imaginations too much . . . do you see what I'm saying? Excess is always negative. Do you feel like drawing a picture?"

"Dunno."

"How about you draw a picture of your family. Doesn't that sound like fun?"

"Can I draw Dad's broken camera?"

"If you want, Casandra. What does putting the camera in your drawing mean for you?"

"She's my best friend."

"'She'? The camera is your imaginary friend?"

"No. But when I grow up, we're going to get married."

"You and the camera?"

"Uh-huh. But not anymore, because now she's dead."

Back then they could still go outside unmonitored, without their father's eyes trailing them from the front door to the curb, tallying their steps. For Dad, staying alive was a question of mathematics and calculated risk. He was a fastidious accountant of all the supposed near assassinations: a bullet in the back, a mine under the moist garden earth, poison in the pizza. Enemies. Culprits. Paranoia. The paranoia you would expect from an important man.

During that period, which was already beginning to fade from Caleb and Casandra's memory, Dad took them to the zoo every Sunday. Calia had not been born yet, of course, and that was for the best, because the animals at the zoo were far from anatomically flawless; they just looked like blots in the distance, smudges with trunks and hooves, whiskers like fabric mustaches, a connect-the-dots puzzle. In those days, animals were just fun blotches and butterflies were just butterflies, not harbingers of death, dark omens on white paper, heralds of imminent damnation born from the mind of their savant sister.

Caleb could still remember those trips to the zoo. He remembered how it felt to love Dad, who did not look as old back then and always wore his medals and his uniform, even on Sundays, because the medals opened every door, even doors that were supposedly unopenable, even the cages at the zoo, those physical representations of the boundary between the higher and lower animals, the victors and vanquished in the battle of evolution. Dad's medals were not pretty, but Caleb was beginning to learn they could be useful.

Casandra only seemed to care about clutching the lens of Dad's Kodak camera, which he let her carry. She would sigh and embrace the camera so forcefully that Caleb thought his sister might plunge it through her dress, that the lens would puncture a round hole in her belly and Casandra would begin taking photos of her insides and spitting prints out her mouth. She caressed the camera with her fingers, steaming up the lens as she sweated her way through our country's endless summer. *My sister's so dumb*, Caleb thought. *If Dad sees, he'll take the camera away for good.* Dad had instructed her to be careful with it, explained that the lens had to be perfectly clean in order to take optimal photos, and it was only after Casandra begged and swore she would be careful that he finally let her hold it for a few minutes.

But in fact, Dad was not watching his daughter at all; he had entirely forgotten about his warning. His priorities were elsewhere. The most important thing was enjoying this outing with his medals and his children. The kids seemed happy and the medals beamed, physical proof that he had a purpose in life, that he was just (or nearly) as important as this country, that he had ascended to heights few ever reached.

"Do you want to see the momomonkeys, Caleb?" he asked his son.

It was a beautiful morning. A magnificent morning. All around, people were hurrying away, heads down, subtly pointing out the medals to one another; a zoo employee followed close behind, ready to do Dad's bidding, anything to please the important man and his family.

Caleb said yes, he wanted to see the monkeys; Dad smiled condescendingly at his son, then looked wordlessly at the zoo employee, a dutiful lackey who practically genuflected in response. Stretching his arm through the bars was not good enough, Caleb said. He wanted to pet the monkeys, hug the monkeys. What, you want me to leave you here all weeweek until you turn into an idiot little momonkey? Dad teased. But Caleb saw that Dad was smiling, so there was no risk in pushing his luck: I wanna pet the monkeys, lemme pet the monkeys! And of course, an important man's boy should have everything his heart desires. Even so, Dad sat him down and said, "Son, take a deep breath. Doodoo you smell something like forbidden rotting fruit? That's the stink of lower mamammals. When you're in there, I only want you pepetting them, not hugging them and getting their stench all over you. Understood?" Dad began making the arrangements: "Cacasandra, give me the camera. I want a phophoto of your brother." Casandra protested and clutched the lens with all her might, but Dad's glare was unyielding. Once he had the camera in hand, he transformed into the important man and barked at the lackey: "You, take my boy to the momonkeys and don't let him get bitten. I'm trusting you." The lackey nodded, tensing so he would not tremble.

Caleb smiled when he saw one of the monkeys approaching. Its swollen belly was big like a balloon about to burst. It stood just a few steps from him and the lackey. That was when Caleb smelled it: not the stink of dry shit or forbidden—rotting—fruit, but a more pungent stench that seemed to come from all around, particularly from the monkey's distended belly.

Caleb barely got to touch it. The monkey collapsed in front of him.

Casandra cried out. Dad took a photo.

"Why are you screaming, Cacasandra? The momomonkey is just taking a nap. It's just a stupid animal."

He turned to the lackey and ordered, "Idiot, doodoo something! Make the stupid momonkey breathe!"

But Caleb knew Dad's wish was impossible. All he had to do was look at the carcass's lifeless eyes. The stench, so potent a moment ago, was gone. That was Caleb's first encounter with fetid death.

Dad took Caleb in his arms. The medals pinched and Caleb cried out.

"Fufufuck, don't cry," Dad said. "It was just a shitty momonkey."

Casandra started crying and demanded the camera back. Caleb felt guilty.

"What happened? Did I do something, Dad?"

"It was just sick, it was going to die ananyway," the important man replied.

Caleb caught another whiff of the smell. Hundreds of whiffs, actually; he could not tell where they were coming from. The stench of death took many forms: for birds it was winged; for fish it was wet, mud-caked, and crusty; it was the smell of a wounded paw; the smell of terminal cancer, metastasis, senescence, a demise long overdue; the smell of that ramshackle, declining zoo; a smell that hovered overhead and surged from beneath the earth; it was in the air, in his mouth. Later, he noticed all the animals trying desperately to approach him, pressing themselves against the bars of their cages, stretching their legs and trunks toward him, fluttering their wings, marching up his father's legs in long, narrow, interminable ranks.

"Fufuck, anananananant's nest!" the man with the medals cried.

"Caleb, what's wrong with you?" Casandra shrieked as a low-flying bird fell dully to the ground, its miniature heart bursting.

Death followed in Caleb's wake: long lines of insect corpses, and the indistinct laments of animals unable to make contact.

I t takes a real woman to give birth without an epidural. Shrieking your way through labor, unsure whether they just excised an organ or pulled a baby from your insides. It is true the misgivings subside with time, as the baby grows and rewards you for the bags under your eyes, the wrinkles, the hopeless saggy tits, the loose skin, the vaginal tearing, the internal and external stitches, the violent obstetricians groping around to extract the blood of your blood and flesh of your flesh. It is true all the pain and agony vanish the first time your child smiles, looks you in the eyes, makes you feel important. Not just important, but like you are, for someone, the only creature in the galaxy that can be equated to the divine principle, string theory, the big bang.

It takes a real woman to give birth, but it takes one hell of a real woman to admit you will never experience what other mothers do in those first hours, days, and months. Not just because the three babies you brought into this world took a big whopping shit inside of you, what the doctors inaptly call fetal distress but ought to call fecal jubilation, the slow splattering of the mother's insides, the fetus's former home, with the foulest of substances; not just because you pumped out three kids with gargantuan heads that forced you to enlarge the episiotomy twice, and not even that was good enough for the third, the breech birth. No, you will never get the same gratification as other mothers because, regardless of gender, each of your kids is a sick son of a bitch.

And that does not make you a bad mother. You tried everything; you even tried loving them, which in the long run turned out to be the hardest. You tried even though they were never especially sweet or intelligent, even though they did not look cute in pictures, even though they were not the product of some epic Hollywood romance. When they came into the world, you promised yourself: I'm going to love them. It'll take work, but I'm going to learn because these are my children, and they will teach me about love in its purest form. Not political fervor or love for medals, not love for Leader Mustache, not love for the homeland we'll defend down to the last man (as the slogan goes), not love of country (a fantasy without a baby's eyes or face), and even though it will be a long, grueling process, I will learn, and they will be by my side, and I will be the world for someone.

But of course, you were wrong. It takes a real woman to accept that her maternal aspirations are a pipe dream. It takes a real woman not to hock a fat loogie at the three shitsacks who fed off you, who never smiled at you, who never loved you, who are wholly immersed in their own selfish priorities, their own miserable lives.

It takes a real woman to conclude that love for your children is not a biological certainty but a learning process that can be thwarted at any moment.

So now you have these three whelps, these three leeches, these three little piggies: Casandra, Caleb, and Calia.

Caca-sandra. Caca-leb. Caca-lia.

The only thing their father got right was the name, that

repetition of the first syllable, his idiot stutter finally serving a purpose: poetic justice.

There is no forgiveness for taking a dump in the womb.

It takes a real woman to look those three in the eyes every night and say:

"Good night, Casandra, my darling."

Caca-sandra, hormonal swine getting off to a bridge or the Berlin Wall.

"Sleep tight, Caleb, my angel."

Caca-leb, angel of death meets Doctor Dolittle.

"See you tomorrow, Calia, my little princess."

Caca-lia, psycho da Vinci freak with the communication skills of a placenta.

And even after all the hypocrisy, after all the emotional labor of carefully enunciating every word without spitting a gob of hot saliva in their ungrateful faces, it takes a real power-house of a woman to endure these three mothershitters who do not look at you, do not talk to you, these three runty cunts to whom you are about as relevant as a soggy filter full of wet coffee grounds.

His whole life he knew he would not die a common death. The certainty was a relief. The pain of death did not concern him. He was prepared to make the ultimate sacrifice for his country and his legacy.

They covered him with medals from shoulder to shoulder. He was a prudent man, a true son of the people. He always had the right words on his lips, and he made sure those words did not escape him, made sure they, the greatest testament to his success, would outlive him in case his medals ever failed or fell silent. But what this prudent man did not realize was that sooner or later, his medals and his words would be condemned to death. Seemingly out of nowhere, the world around him began to collapse.

He had unfailingly complied with protocol. There was not a man alive who could point a finger at him. When his country needed soldiers, he fought. When Leader Mustache needed a defender, he spoke up. And when the enemies of the people needed to be dealt with, who stepped up, who embraced the gruesome responsibility of asking questions and administering pain? We all know the answer: orders exist because men like him live to carry them out. And, of course, Dad considered himself a hero—an aging one perhaps, with fatigue in his bones, but a hero nevertheless—who intended to remain standing.

Dad knows that power is not given: it is won or lost.

And his time to lose had come.

In the language of politics, loss and disgrace are synonyms, and Dad was so fluent in that language that when he talked about medals, wars, and the triumphs of yesteryear, it was impossible to know whose story he was telling, impossible to distinguish between history, faded memories, and fictions conjured up from the circumstances of his own tragedy. This was fortuitous, as it forced Dad to become a kind of storytelling grandmother who could transform tales of war into sweet lullabies, canonizing his own military grandeur as classical mythology. At first, he repeated his stories, but before long, he had mastered the art of adaptation. Dad was a prudent man, the epitome of persistence. He learned to spice up his storylines, to mix and match, pulling twists and turns and new characters from his sleeve. The latest and greatest in narrative innovation, narrative bodywork. And when he had crafted the perfect hulking antagonist, with nine hairy legs, a deformed ear, and medals pinned to his chest—because the monster, too, had been a man of his time—Dad was satisfied. He had constructed an epic in his own image and likeness, forged a nation with his own molds.

He considered himself a man of his time, just as important, or nearly as important, as Leader Mustache, who, it was important not to forget, really should not be called that, just like he should not be affectionately referred to as Pop-Pop Mustache. That was presumptuous familiarity, childish impertinence. In military life, anyone who alluded to the General's mustache or gave him an affectionate nickname would have gotten a beating. "General Mustache" was not as bad, since at least it mentioned his rank, no small thing, but even so, it struck Dad as an exercise in indiscipline—that most reckless strain of vulgarity. Why bring up the General's mustache at all? To mock his appearance? To mock his elegant facial hair, which the General preferred to morphological frontal balding? Is a mustache really so uncommon that it qualifies as a defining feature? Dad understood that it was critical to think twice and look both ways before talking about the General, before speaking a single syllable. Denigrating the General's lifestyle, physical appearance, or decisions was a serious matter. The most serious of all. Especially now, in this new era in which the family had fallen into disgrace.

As a man of his time, he established strict laws for his entire household. A sort of court martial minus the trials. He took Casandra aside. She was the oldest of his children and she had a habit of talking about the General in overly familiar terms. Pop-Pop Mustache. Uncle Mustachio. Old Man Whiskers. Mustaches flew thoughtlessly from Casandra's brazen lips, and with them, the implication of wrongdoing that could fall into the wrong hands; all information was valuable now that the family was observed like bacteria under a microscope. God forbid Casandra's words be overheard by some hairy, seditious ear, an ear attached to a body that did not have medals on its chest like Dad, or that, if it did have medals on its chest, did not deserve them. Dad's years in politics had proven only one law to be true: a man of His Time, a man willing to make the ultimate sacrifice for His Time, is not born every day.

"Look, Cacasandra, you're practically a young wowoman now and you should know the truth . . ." The speech had been extensively planned, syllable by syllable; every word had a purpose. Dad lowered his voice to almost a whisper. "Will you doodoo what I say, Cacasandra?"

"Depends." She yawned. "Is it something boring?"

Dad resisted the urge to smack his smart-mouthed daughter across the face. Otherwise, they might later say that military men were violent in their domestic lives, that they established dictatorships in their own homes. What if they made a documentary about him one day? About his heroic life? But Dad knew expectations could be dangerous, so he rewound the tape in his head, decided it would be preferable for them to make a documentary about General Mustache, in which, perhaps, Cacasandra, Cacaleb, and Cacalia would have the chance, in their moment of stardom, to tell some relatable, amusing family anecdote about him, dear old Dad, a man of his time, always prepared to defend the General by rifle or rhetoric. In Dad's imagination, the anecdotes would not be frivolous; the children would add that he was a kind father who never raised a hand against his unruly son or daughters, who took them to the zoo every Sunday, who gave his firstborn countless broken camera lenses for her bizarre collection, who supported the baby's selective mutism. He was a man of his time, the children would say in the documentary, but he was also a father of his time: gentle, kind, democratic, warm, engaged, concerned with his children's welfare. Him, smack his smart-ass cunt freak pervert bitch daughter across the face? Never.

Dad smiled. "No, it's not boring at all, it's a nenew law that will enter into force in our fafafamily."

Casandra yawned and shrugged. "Okay, hurry up."

"Pop-Pop Mustache . . . saying that is a bad habit. I don't

know how to mamake you understand. From now on we'll call him our Supr, our Susupr, our Sususupr—"

"We'll call him our supper?"

"Our Supreme Leader! Do you understand?"

"Uh-huh."

"Cacasandra, this isn't a joke."

"I know, I know what's happening."

"What do you mememean you know 'what's happening'?"

"They're gonna take your medals away, right?"

"Nonononono."

"They're not?" Cacasandra made a face. "You must've done something really bad to piss off Pop-Pop Mustache. I mean, he always looks angry in pictures, but in real life he's really nice, and people say . . ."

"Don't believe everything peepeepeople say!"

"Okay."

Dad loved her. That is, he loved all three of them, all three of his little mistakes. But sometimes it was difficult. Sometimes he had to remind himself that men of their time were called upon to be both democratic fathers and unyielding soldiers. Governing the nation was one thing and raising his three failed genetic experiments was another. Was he disappointed? Obviously. He had dreamed of breeding heroic children who would inherit his best physical features and his remarkable propensity for leadership, as well as the other moral qualities that should have made them worthy of bearing one of the most important surnames in the country. But the genetic lottery is rigged. What else could you expect from a mediocre ovum and an over-stressed spermatozoon? They were destined for failure. Three consecutive failures, in fact.

Cacasandra, for example, was the firstborn letdown and the most painful. Cacaleb was less bothersome, but he was always just *around*, lost, perhaps, in his own thoughts. And do not even get him started on Cacalia. Cacalia was a world unto herself, and Dad knew it was a very complex world, brimming with watercolor elephants, oil-paint elephants, crayon elephants, all anatomically correct; a zoological Crayola highway on which he was not even allowed to thumb a ride because there were no trucks, no taxis, no motorcycles; it was a highway free of air and noise pollution, free of everything except Cacalia and her animals, and they braked for no hitchhiker.

Despite her status as firstborn letdown, Cacasandra was still the child with whom he felt closest; she was the only one capable of approximating a normal child's behavior, though this always came battered in the whisked egg and breadcrumbs of pseudosagacity, the affected wisdom of a teenager searching for fancy words to spit in her parents' faces. Cacasandra was unruly and Dad meant nothing to her, and it is important to note that Dad knew this, felt this in his bones. He was overwhelmed every time he stepped into his daughter's bedroom, which was covered floor-to-ceiling in photos of the Eiffel Tower, the Sagrada Familia, bridge after bridge, photo after photo of buildings and infrastructure from every possible angle. His daughter the pervert, his daughter the architect, in the throes of teenage fixation.

"Doodoo you want me to get angry, Cacasandra? Answer me popolitely, please. Don't just say okay."

"Super."

"Don't say susuper either."

"I can't say super and I can't say Pop-Pop Mustache?"

"No, nothing to do with mumustaches. Or with popopop-pops or uncles or anything like that. He's Our Leader."

"Our supper."

"Our Supreme Leader, or the General."

Cacasandra smirked. "I'm gonna miss Pop-Pop Mustache. He always used to bring me dolls."

"And for the record, no one's taking away my mememe-medals."

"Super. Lucky you. Can you imagine if they did? It'd be like they chopped off your arms and legs. Or worse."

Cacasandra was right. Better a mutilated freak than a man without a legacy, a man without a country, a man not of his time.

"Keep your voice down, Cacasandra, they'll hear us," Dad reproached. "There are mimicrophones everywhere."

"Maybe, I guess." Cacasandra laughed. "But you wouldn't know. It wouldn't matter anyway. I don't think anyone's interested in listening to what you say."

Fucking bitch. Fucking teenager. Adolescent and idiot were synonyms as far as he was concerned.

"I'm a ma . . . I'm a ma . . . I'm a mama . . . I'm a mamaman of great importance!"

"Sure, sure. But you're on Pop-Pop Mustache's . . . on our supper's shit list now, aren't you? You're . . . what do they call it? Collateral damage. Tell me honestly, what did you do?"

"Nonothing!"

"Nothing at all? No way."

"It was all them, not mememe!"

"Ah, my aunt and uncle . . ."

Dad bit his lip. "What do you know about your aunt and uncle? What do you know, Cacasandra?"

"Aren't they traitors?"

Dad bit his lip again, harder this time. He said nothing.

"They tried to kill Pop-Pop Mustache," Cacasandra said with a shrug. "No wonder he's pissed."

There is whispering in the corners and unease in the air, penetrating her lungs' minute alveoli with the smell of the living. It does not matter. Calia knows better than to think about the outside world, where the supposedly higher mammals have gathered under the same roof, where, out of genetic custom, they call one another family. More important is finishing the elephant hoof she is drawing. But that is not the hard part. The hard part comes next: the hairs on its trunk. Calia sweats. The flies land on her skin. To see if the drawing of the hairs turns out lifelike, if the hairs seem to quiver with the elephant's every inhalation. Hairs that do not quiver are anything but hairs. She grips the pen and stills her hand. Matters of anatomy are an exercise in relaxation. Calia repeatedly counts backward, summons the image of a lotus opening just there, neither to the left nor to the right, but just at the center of her forehead—*blossom, lotus*—so her hand does not shake, so the hairs she draws are hairs and not butterflies, so it is hairs and not butterflies fluttering in the wind. Calia is annoyed, she does not understand why she is picturing colorful insects when the task at hand is not one of aesthetics, but of precision, why she feels those wings flapping just above the golden lotus. *Blossom, golden lotus; be gone, butterfly; fly, butterfly, away from the fucking lotus.* It is difficult to concentrate with her mother outside. Calia recognizes her, the fattest of the higher mammals in her inaptly termed family. Mom says Calia's name, tries to get her attention and to close the golden lotus—*fuck off, lotus*—there is no way out, there is no escaping Mom's call for attention, so Calia looks up. There stands the fat mammal, and Calia looks without seeing its face until she notices—*how curious; blossom, golden lotus*—that her mother has hairs in her nose, long elephant hairs, hyperrealistic hairs that undulate—*blossom, lotus*—and quiver with her every inhalation. *Just as the elephant's must.* And the recurring thought strikes again: *Do butterflies have hairs*, she wonders. But the butterflies vanish abruptly because the external noise emitted from the trunk—that is, from the supposedly higher mammal's nasopharyngeal apparatus directly in front of Calia—muffles everything.

"So, what are we drawing today, princess?" Mom asks.

Close, lotus, the magic is over, lotus.

Calia becomes bored, so bored, whenever the mammal speaks. They are not normal words, but a more complicated thing called therapy. *Die, lotus, fuck off, lotus.* Calia keeps looking at the hairs; it would be good to know why this herd of supposedly evolved animals observes her so closely. Maybe they like her elephants. What would the family do if they realized Calia cannot tolerate them?

It is possible to look at it from another angle. For example, a purportedly higher mammal capable of speech would never deign to chat with a caterpillar. From this example—*blossom, lotus*—it is easy to draw conclusions: Calia, *Homo sapiens generabilis*, does not deign to converse with the simple hominids. It is not a question of inability or adaptation; language is useful, words are useful for communication between members of the same species, but how foul to squander saliva on *Homo sapiens* *vulgaris—sigh, lotus—*even if it is part of the protocol. Calia knows the protocol and knows that the family, those relations with which indiscriminate genetics has haphazardly saddled her—*blossom, lotus—*worry about her speech and language development milestones. And this gets in her way.

Mom, the mammal with the long nose hairs, speaks again:

"Calia, darling, tell me the truth."

And then, aghast:

"Flies! Flies everywhere! I'll swat them off you! They're all over you, Calia!"

Fly wings.

"All I want is for you to tell me the truth. Tell me if it's you, if you're in there." Her mother's voice sounds raw.

Calia starts drawing faster.

Butterfly wings.

'm gonna talk about love, okay? That's what you expect from a teenager telling a story that's at least partially about herself. It's a matter of hormones and geographic location. Of being a storyteller and a witness. Though, when it comes to love, I wouldn't be much of a witness, no. To talk about love, you need to have seen it from an impartial, third-person point of view, omniscient, omnisapient, omnicogent, maybe even omnignorant. We know that every child in history came from blitzing hormones, biological needs, and aspirations to immortality in a blender, sometimes with the addition of a secret ingredient. That secret ingredient, as many of you will have guessed, is love. But it's an ingredient rarely found in nature. It only appears once in a blue moon and never stays for long. Still with me? Everything okay? Super. This time frame can be so tight that it only materializes at the beginning of a relationship or during its most famous squabbles, meaning it's unlikely a kid will get conceived in that window, in that narrow opening where the secret ingredient flowers and flourishes.

It's super unlikely I was the product of a harmonious union between my parents. Right? There was never any love there. Or if there was, the kitchen ran out of its secret ingredient a long way back. It's hard, I know. Love is hard. Who in the fuck could put up with Mom's therapizing. Who in the fuck could put up with Dad's medals.

So, we're gonna start from a place of ignorance, okay?

I'm gonna talk about love, but my way. So come with me, and together we'll blitz this juicy salad into a tasty shit smoothie, because not everything we serve up in this kitchen is pretty or to everyone's liking.

I remember my first time.

Who doesn't?

To talk about love, you have to talk about the object of your affection. Because in every other respect, romance is pretty much the same. Still with me? Super. It's easier this way. I say love and you know what I'm talking about, no need for metaphors. The variable is the object. That is, *what* we fall in love with.

I said *what*.

Understand?

For me, it isn't a *what*. Or not just a *what*. Okay? I know, I get it, it doesn't breathe, it's not the same as you, or Cacaleb, or Cacalia, but it's not as dead as the creatures my brother kills either. Let's just say its breathing is *different*. Its breathing is a vibration. A secret vibration. You follow?

No? Lost?

I'm talking about love. About the object of love. About the first object of my desire.

My father started photographing us. For a while, he was obsessed. An important man ought to have a graphic archive of his own life and of his progeny's. That's where we came into the frame. Dad made us wear costumes, get dressed up like sailors, soldiers, miners, gnomes; in formalwear; in bathing suits for a fake beach we never went to; our Sunday best, our Monday best, our Wednesday best; smile, Cacasandra, stay there,

Cacaleb, he'd say, and later, when Cacalia came on the scene, we included her in our photo shoots even though she put up a fight, she didn't fit in the frame and wasn't fond of dressing up like a little sailor or a little soldier, c'mon Cacalia, smile, c'mon Cacalia, look here. But Cacalia was the same as she is today, always lost in her drawings, in her monkey-butt period, focused on every veiny, spongy detail, her hyperrealistic touches, and Dad had no choice but to force her to join the circle with her siblings, click, click, click, Cacaleb with his obedient face and me with an expression of unadulterated ardor.

Because it's true, I had fallen in love, the object of my affection was hanging from Dad's neck, witnessing me in my sailor costume and my red bow, or in my blue bow and ruffled swimsuit.

It was love at first sight.

Or at least at first photo.

Beautiful, Cacasandra, Dad praised my smile, and he beamed with pride at the daughter who wasn't a disappointment for once, who fit into his dream of immortality by way of photography. But I wasn't doing it for him, I was doing it for *it*.

Okay? Following? Do we all understand?

My first love was Dad's camera.

It was a matter of focus. Or of lens. I fell in love with the lens. Its roundness, the way it opened like a flower. It was cold and smelled like something unusual, like plastic and glass. Even today I remember that smell. It has evolved into other, more complex scents, like the smell of rust on old bridges, limescale on a building, the wood of a chair. It was short-lived yet passionate with the chair, but we'll get to that later. For now, we'll keep our impulses in check and go into the past, rewind the tape, roll back the film.

Back to the camera.

My favorite photos were the ones without my siblings. Solitary photos gave me the chance to contemplate the object of my love and to be contemplated in return. Dad smiled, proud. And I trembled. Butterflies in my stomach. No, not butterflies, what if Calia found out? Bugs in my stomach, fluttering.

Secret love is a bittersweet blend of frustration and hormones, you know? Of course, back then I couldn't describe it. I didn't know terms like dopamine (which addled my brain and wouldn't let me sleep), separation anxiety, angst. I just waited, yearning for the moment Dad would remember his compulsion to document reality; he was overjoyed that I was part of it, that I wanted to be part of the story. If Cacalcb protested or Cacalia refused to participate, I was always there, smiling and ready for my close-up, over and over, willing to do anything for the object of my affection. I was so obedient that sometimes Dad let me touch the camera lens.

Happiness is a diffuse form that even today I associate with the act of gazing upon what you love, and being gazed upon in return.

I already told you this is a love story, okay? Just maybe not your typical boy-meets-girl, boy-meets-boy, girl-meets-girl.

I have loved walls that were demolished. Those were the most terrible loves, something between the platonic ideal and the feeling that you were born after your time. I loved a dishwasher once. It was brief, a two-month affair. It didn't feel mutual, I had to let it go. And I have loved buildings. A tower. It's true I had a fling with a chair, or maybe it was just a spark, something that never came to full fruition, but it still forms part of my consummated erotic fantasies. There's something about pieces of antique furniture, an indefinable quality, I guess it's their years of experience; a big age difference is always arousing.

These are the objects of my love.

Still with me? So, yes: this is a love story about teenage frustration, hormones, and a secret ingredient. Okay?

Don't say I didn't warn you.

Pop-Pop Mustache used to arrive out of the blue, unannounced. Whoever said unexpected visitors were a nuisance? Of course not! It was a joy every time Pop-Pop Mustache stepped through the door. Dad's nerves would fire on all cylinders, manifesting as sweat droplets sliding down his neck, his forehead; nerves were his greatest enemy, so Dad wrang his hands. Being a faithful man of his time, dutybound to the General and the General's whiskers, involved tremendous effort, especially if the General was in his home, breaching the sphere of repose and privacy where everything was strange, a place where one could usually stutter with abandon, unconcerned with what other men with medals might say, and especially unconcerned with the children's eccentricities, which they possessed in spades and which had to be concealed from Pop-Pop Mustache at all costs.

If the General ever noticed those eccentricities, he did not seem to care. He burst into the house with his boots covered in dust, but he shook his feet as he entered and called out:

"Now, my little Casandrita, where did you disappear to?" and as he looked for the hiding child—part of a longstanding pact between Pop-Pop Mustache and Casandra, not yet a teenager—the General smiled and rubbed his palms together.

He never showed up empty-handed.

The instant he came inside, Pop-Pop Mustache became the

host. Never mind that it was not his house; when it came down to it, it was his country, and that house, within his country, formed just another small part of his expansive domain. Everyone was to play by his rules and everyone knew it. The bodyguards remained outside, as this was before the aunt and uncle tried to assassinate Pop-Pop Mustache. He was in friendly territory; a safe space, the peace-loving home of a man of his time, loyal to his country, to Pop-Pop Mustache, and to the notion of a perfect, functional family unit.

The aging General struck Casandra as comical: tall and ungainly, somehow lanky at one moment and fleshy another. And he always pointed at everything, as if indicating which things he deemed important and which were expendable. He poked his finger at all of it, including the medals on Dad's chest.

"Remind me again, soldier, when did I give you that medal?"

"Two years ago, General."

"Ah yes, two, hmm, and what'd I give it to you for?"

Dad launched into a lengthy, slightly absurd story involving the underpinnings of his merit with such a wealth of detail that Pop-Pop Mustache grew bored.

"Yes, yes . . . I remember," he lied.

He liked coffee. No sugar. And sweets as sweet as could be. A man of contrasts. The most charming thing about him was, indeed, the eponymous mustache, which was neither too short nor too long, neither neglected nor excessively groomed. The General's mustache was an expression of balance, you might call it Grecian balance, which, as everyone knows, or at least ought to know, means proper measure in all things. The General's mustache could be described as regal, classical, Socratic, the only perfect thing about his body. The rest was perfectly mediocre. Even his uniform left much to be desired. It was immaculate early in the morning, but as the hours passed, it wrinkled, bunched up here and there, filled with hand- or fist-prints depending on the General's mood that particular day.

Casandra was fascinated with the mustache.

"Come here, Casandrita. Sit right here, . . ." the General would say, making himself comfortable as he smoked a cigarette and sipped bitter coffee.

Casandra did not mind the smoke, but Pop-Pop Mustache always put his cigarette out anyway.

"Guess what I've brought for you."

She did not have to think hard.

"A doll."

"You're smarter every time I see you, Casandrita."

It did not take much smarts to know Pop-Pop Mustache loved giving dolls as gifts. Over the years, Casandra had received them in every shape and size.

"There's nothing better than dolls of all kinds," he always said, beaming with a childlike love of toys.

He delighted in Casandra. This was the secret pact between them. She set her dolly court up around Pop-Pop Mustache and he kneeled beside her, listening attentively to her make-believe orders: *Dolly, stop being a brat and finish your dinner. What, you're not hungry? Then you're grounded. Dolly, what's the matter with you? Why won't you look me in the eyes? Dolly, it's time for you to grow up already.* And so on, the output of her churlish imagination on full display before the General, all so she could see his perfect Grecian mustache. Meanwhile, Dad strained to join the conversation at all costs, to insert himself into the dynamic between the General and his daughter. It was a good opportunity for a right-hand man to present himself as a family man, practically Pop-Pop Mustache's next of kin. He bloviated, blustered, and stuttered away as the General absently agreed, nodding into the void. Casandra wondered why Pop-Pop Mustache put up with her idiot father.

When the General grew tired of Dad's relentless, obsequious chatter, he would wave his hand, a gesture that said, *I'm bored*, a motion that required no words to be considered an order, inexorable and definitive like an execution. If he was in a good mood, Pop-Pop Mustache would add:

"At ease, soldier. Try to cherish your daughter a little. She'll grow up before you know it."

Casandra was quicker. Sharper than Dad. Little by little, she had secured a seat for herself on Pop-Pop Mustache's knees. That was a privilege afforded only to very special children, the ones they put on TV to commemorate important dates or when the General wanted to present himself as the Father of the People. Those children were vetted, specially cast to represent the diversity of the nation in all its colors and shapes. But Casandra knew she was even more special than the children on TV and in the interviews because she lived in the real world where he was not the General, but Pop-Pop Mustache.

"Why do you have a mustache?" she once asked.

Dad shot daggers at his daughter. He spoke her name in a loud, scandalized voice, and Casandra pretended to cower, feigned genuine fear, enough for the General to click his tongue with disapproval and shoot daggers of his own at Dad. Now Dad felt what it was like to be reprimanded, and of course, he did not like it. Everyone feared a click of Pop-Pop Mustache's tongue.

"Well, it's because mustaches are very interesting," he replied to the girl.

"Interesting?"

"And mysterious. No one can ever be quite certain, for example, if I'm laughing. Or, if I'm annoyed and press my lips together, the mustache hides that too. Mustaches are like a mask. Do you know what a mask is, Casandrita?"

She did, but she shook her head.

"Masks are a weapon. All intelligent men should have at least one."

"So Dad isn't intelligent?"

The General laughed, choking on his own spit.

"Kids these days," he said, and though he was responding to Casandra's question, he turned to give Dad a derisive look. "Believe me, it's much better that your father is clean-shaven."

"Why?"

"What a good question. The truth is, I don't like copycats. And anyone who tries to copy me is doomed to fail."

At that, Dad trembled for some strange reason, and Casandra felt powerful, very powerful, in fact, because Pop-Pop Mustache seemed to love her more than he loved Dad and Dad's medals. He could not recall when or why he had given Dad all those medals, but he remembered the name of each of Casandra's dolls and the exact day he had given them to her.

"Can I call you Pop-Pop?" Casandra asked.

"Why shouldn't you?" The General smiled, almost tenderly.

"My Pop-Pop Mustache?"

The General did not reply, but Casandra knew perfectly well the look of an adult moved by emotion.

That knowledge was a weapon too.

The flies continued to proliferate in the summer heat.

Summer was the original pupa from which all flies emerged.

Ever since Dad's medals lost their effect and Pop-Pop Mustache stopped visiting the house, new laws had gone into effect for every member of the family, strictly enforced.

"It was all a misunderstanding," Dad spat as he wrang his hands with arrhythmic jitters. "The General is fair. He can't put me in the same cacamp as those unpatriotic didididissidents."

The unpatriotic dissidents were the children's aunt and uncle.

The unpatriotic dissidents were also the only normal people Caleb had met in his life. It is true he did not have a great baseline for comparison, since the closest thing to normalcy at home was Mom, an avid collector of self-help and group-therapy books whose hatred for her three children created a dense atmosphere that Caleb was sure even the flies could detect if they cared to try.

The other members of the family, well, Caleb preferred not to talk about them. They did not seem to realize how freakish they were, which only complicated things. *Awareness of your own freakishness is the first step toward family tolerance*, Caleb thought. Meanwhile, the sick and elderly flies continued to land on his skin, and of course we already know their intention. Even flies have a clear purpose in life, the common thread across all of creation: to die without pain. And Caleb was their pill, their palliative, their passage to housefly paradise, an idyllic place with interminable rows of trash cans to land upon. Caleb was the fountain of death. At least he was aware of his own freakishness and took due precaution. He understood he was a passport to nonexistence and tried to conceal this fact so he could seem a little more normal; from the animals, he learned the value of camouflage. The image of Casandra's eyes at the zoo that day was burned in his memory, along with Dad's disappointment, and most of all, the dead animals, the creatures that had reached out with the hope, or something akin to hope, of making contact and ending the agony of their incarceration. It was not the last time. Later came a rabbit, a turtle, and flies, infinite flies with lumpy legs, missing wings, sticky from succumbing to water, damp, and dying, distressing processions of bugs bent on death. When Caleb tried to keep his distance, it was even worse; the insects forced their way to him, they were persistent, you had to admire it, persistence is a virtue not limited to the human species. Mendicant caravans of creepy-crawlies hounded Caleb until he finally relented with a stroke of mercy—*suffer no more*—and a stroke of worldly self-consciousness to be expected from a boy so young—*but you have to quit making me suffer too or everybody'll know I'm a freak*. Let the dying creatures come, he conceded, and convoys of flies, ants, crickets, cockroaches approached in shameless pursuit of their own demise; the creatures were sensible to the blessing that boy's body could bestow, the blessing of a peaceful death.

It was not always possible for Caleb to hide, despite his best efforts at camouflage. Often he had to surrender. At school, for example. What could he do on the playground, surrounded by fresh grass, to stop the relentless parade of ennui-stricken ants from climbing toward his knees. How could he possibly have known that his sister's rabbit had terminal cancer rotting it from the inside, that the rabbit was in agonizing distress, that it no longer nibbled at lettuce, that it did nothing but gaze at the world through a glassless window, until one day Caleb touched it, innocent and guileless, certainly without meaning to put the animal out of a misery he was not even aware of—the only giveaway was how, whenever he walked past, the bunny hopped frantically, pressed hard against the bars of its cage. Looking back with the benefit of enlightened retrospection, the signals were clear. But back then, Caleb did not see them: all he saw was a bunny he thought was cute; in fact, he was sure it was female, and pregnant, hence the round belly, the swelling that grew worse with every passing day. Anything pregnant, regardless of species, eventually grows large and convex. How was Caleb supposed to know it wasn't a baby bunny but cancer making the rabbit swell, how was he supposed to know that cancer gestates too, but differently, painfully. He petted the bunny, finally, on a day like any other. The cage briefly shuddered the instant his fingers grazed the animal's snout. That was the whole episode. There is nothing else to tell except Casandra's screams. *Bunnykiller Caleb* was the best epithet she could come up with on the spot. "I hate you," she cried—strong words, though she did not cry—"I hate you, Bunnykiller Caleb."

"Cacaleb, what did you do?" Dad asked. "Why?" The questions lingered in the air, dangling like carrots.

The autopsy on the pet's distended body was no great help. That was back when Dad's medals were still good for something, still served a purpose; each symbolized an order that would be executed to the letter, and if Dad said rabbit autopsy, his wish was their command. The rabbit was opened and each of its organs painstakingly analyzed. Who knows, better safe than sorry. Enemies of the people could have poisoned the children's pet somehow, they do that sort of thing all the time, Dad said, there are enemies of the people lurking around every corner, willing to resort to terrorist methods. They don't just lob bombs, bombs are child's play for enemies of the people, they're far more inventive than that, they employ creative and convoluted tactics, for example poisoning a rabbit with uranium or some other radioactive substance. An autopsy would give the death a face, a face that was not Caleb's, since, according to Dad, even the oddest phenomena have a dialectical explanation that obeys the laws of nature. Who would believe the boy possessed rabbit-killing, insect-murdering power. No—radioactive uranium, enemies of the people, these were words familiar to Dad, words from the handbook, which he knew by heart, and which made as much sense to him as the weight of his medals.

The word "cancer" was also comprehensible. Just two syllables. Easy. That is that. The rabbit, which was a male, died of a painful, terminal disease. It was better this way. Dad said something along those lines to an enraged Casandra, and for consolation, he gave her a new camera lens, at which point his daughter forgot everything and became fully engrossed in her new game.

"Cacaleb," Dad said a few days later, capitalizing on a moment alone with his son. "Whawhat did you do to that rabbit? Tell the truth."

"Nothing."

"You totouched it and it died? Just like that?"

"Yeah, on its nose."

"Did you kick it on its nonose?"

"No."

"Wawawas it like that time at the zoo?"

"Yeah."

"Shit, Cacaleb. Don't tell anyone. Remember, there are enenemies of the people lurking around every corner and they'll use any information they cacan get their hands on against us."

Dad did not say or ask anything else. He just went to polish or fondle his medals. To calm himself down.

Caleb thought about enemies of the people a lot. There seemed to be so many of them lurking around every corner. A mathematical equation: the greater Dad's importance, the more enemies of the people threatened the family. Conclusion: now that Dad had problems, the number of enemies of the people ought to drop, right? Caleb also thought about his aunt and uncle. Associative property. His aunt and uncle, who were normal, had become some kind of peculiar monster. No one even said their names anymore, at least not loudly. *She*—third-person feminine singular—was his aunt. *He*—third-person masculine singular—was his uncle. The apt use of *they*—third-person plural—encompassed the union of those two particular enemies of the people who had brought disgrace upon Dad.

It was hard to understand exactly what Dad's disgrace involved. That was not discussed aloud either. Television had been banned, at least for the time being. There was no radio in the house, and the newspapers had not arrived in weeks. The outside world had closed like an oyster. And although they had not stripped Dad of his medals, something was happening, clearly, because Pop-Pop Mustache had stopped visiting and Dad's stutter was getting worse:

"She . . . she didididid it." He was referring to Caleb's aunt, third-person feminine singular. "And he's her kikikikiss-ass sycophant."

Caleb's aunt and uncle were normal people. She liked to sew. He liked making spaghetti. They had two kids. All of them wore glasses. There is nothing more normal than people who wear glasses. Caleb could not imagine an enemy of the people wearing glasses.

It was too ordinary.

The butterfly fixation began years earlier, when Mom was still a girl. Back then, most topics were discussed in hushed tones. Raising your voice was a privilege because the walls had ears, including the neighbors' walls, which were the most dangerous walls of all. No one could be trusted, and secrets had to be kept under double lock and double key. Mom was just a kid back then, but she already understood raising your voice was an act of rebellion, and if she asked a question, if she wanted to know what the grown-ups at the table were talking about, she would receive the standard responses: children speak when hens piss gold, children ask questions when frogs grow hairs, children have opinions when barracudas fly, and these natural phenomena, so different from other phenomena kid-Mom was familiar with, were so odd that she never dared fantasize about understanding anything.

Still, over time she learned—or more precisely inferred, read between the sloppily stitched lines—what the adults were talking about, decoded words and gleaned concepts.

When it came to natural phenomena, Mom could talk for hours.

For example, she could talk about her beautiful aunt, her silent spinster aunt, the one with the huge ass, the artist who had not stopped drawing since she was two years old, the one who—according to kid-Mom's grandmother, who was also this aunt's mother—had never spoken a word. That is, her Aunt Juliana, whom they had to leave alone to parley with God the only way she knew how, with Crayola crayons, because that was her lot in this world. The beautiful aunt was allowed to draw all she wanted. And look how good at it she was. A genius. A genius committed to capturing animal morphology with anatomical precision. It was a shame that the beautiful aunt was not also committed to making money, because then they would be millionaires. Who would not want a framed elephant that was practically alive? Who would not want monkeys, whales, parrots, salamanders that seemed to breathe? But kid-Mom's grandmother—the silent aunt's mother—understood that Juliana had to be left alone to parley with God, don't bother her, what do you want to sell her art for anyway, she's happy, the important thing is your aunt is happy, she's not interested in us, we aren't intelligent enough for her. This claim struck kid-Mom as outrageous, but she did not say anything, she just sat alone with her thoughts. No one could stop her from thinking; she was queen of her own thought-palace, a place where the hens pissed riches, the frogs grew thick coats of fur, and the barracudas took to the skies. Kid-Mom knew the truth: Aunt Juliana can't stand us, we just get in her way, one day they'll see I'm right, kid-Mom convinced herself, all you have to do is look her in the eyes for a second and right away you see it, you can spot it a mile away, she is the master of us all.

The real natural phenomenon came later.

The beautiful aunt started drawing butterflies.

Day after day.

From dusk to dawn.

I've always loved butterflies, sighed kid-Mom's grandmother

who was also, as has already been repeatedly indicated, the silent spinster aunt's mother.

With the butterfly drawings, everything began to change. Including her silent aunt, who that day spoke for the first time:

"Now our death begins," said the aunt, at which point everyone in the house reacted with applause, thunderous applause like falling stones, and in that moment no one paused to consider the specific, macabre words the aunt had selected. Because, hey, people die every day, don't they? The miracle here, the miracle was that the butterfly lady had finally spoken after her lengthy tête-à-tête with God. Now that conversation was over, and God was prepared to use the aunt's mouth as a vehicle. Because it is true, the aunt was no longer silent, she was simply a beautiful woman with oversize eyes.

t sounds like a hog brought to slaughter. Mom recognizes the moans of her swine daughter, the pervert slut whose name bears the fecal prefix, and she feels an overwhelming urge to kick down the door. There is nothing worse than the sound of someone else's orgasm when you yourself have no orgasms. Mom knows merely from having birthed her truculent eldest daughter that she does it on purpose, that her swine child masturbates behind the shelter of the bedroom door to provoke her. Every afternoon Casandra waits for her father to leave for the outside world, where he does God knows what. Meanwhile, in the kingdom of her own home, Mom does not listen to, field questions from, or demand answers from her own consciousness; the fact of the matter is that Cacasandra's father, bestower of the fecal prefix, has a life of his own beyond the domestic borders, beyond his wife's knowledge, beyond the orgasms his wife has not had, and beyond the unsatisfying few she has. That is all the merit that can be conferred upon the man with the medals.

There is nothing sophisticated about Casandra's disdain for her mother: it is fairly rudimentary, an almost therapeutic scorn for authority figures, Mom thinks, especially for female authority figures, and the scorn manifests as confrontation. That perfectly explains the cynicism, the hormonal swine face, the moans, the guilty glean in her duplicitous eyes when she throws open the bedroom door so her splendid postorgasmic glow can be celebrated by one and all. It's a stupid, transparent, adolescent ploy to incite maternal spite or envy, a classic case of therapeutic contempt, it's textbook really, and easily treatable if Cacasandra would ever take therapy seriously.

Cacasandra strives to moan loud and hard, she is a clever hog who always opts to touch herself during the exact hours her father is out, it is curious, this adolescent loathing, this gambit to get the better of her mother, pathological Cacasandra, logical Cacasandra.

Mom knocks carefully on the bedroom door. Gently, but loud enough to interrupt the moan and spoil the orgasm.

"Casandra . . . ?"

Neutral tone, subtle and unassuming. This would be enough to curb her swine daughter if she were not what she is, a brazen bitch who loves nothing more than her own ecstatic cries, who wants her mother submissive before the unsavory sound.

For a few minutes, Mom remains beside the door and waits for a response of any kind. Casandra could at least cobble together some sort of excuse. Barring that, she could at least quiet down, fall into the ashamed silence of a child who knows that antagonizing her mother is a grave miscalculation, a mistake of the highest order. But it is useless, Cacasandra's moans carry on unabated, a rudimentary case of contempt for her mother, a Trojan contempt, Grecian even, both ancient and classic, befitting her name.

It is not the first time Mom has heard Casandra moaning. No matter what her daughter thinks, Mom can, in fact, remember and identify the sound. Now that Mom is thinking about it, she realizes there is a trace of suspicion in Casandra's contempt: I wonder if Mom can recognize cries of pleasure—her daughter must be thinking—or if to her they'll just sound like a hand polishing medals, because it's only when he's polishing medals that Dad has a hand and a body, only then that he's a man of his time, when he's far from Mom, a woman who has clearly already served her biological purpose of breeding and birthing progeny. Her uterus is just interim housing for the children, her vagina is just a birth canal, best to avoid touching Mom's pleasure anatomy, better to pretend it doesn't exist, never existed, since it has no role in upholding his notions of genetic immortality.

Yes, of course Mom remembers what cries of pleasure sound like, even if her daughter thinks of her as nothing but an incubator, an egg-laying hen, an ovum dispenser. Mom could touch herself. Mom could have orgasms if she wanted. Mom convinces herself of this and her mood immediately brightens: Why bother confronting her daughter's sexual vulgarity with vulgarity of her own, why breed more therapeutic contempt, where is the value in proving that? If she liked, she could easily be the orgasm queen in this house, in this domain. Her domain—not that swine Cacasandra's.

Mom prefers to wait behind the door, listening to her daughter, who is in turn listening to her: a scene of bilateral sonic espionage.

"Casandrita . . . ?" Mom knocks treacherously as the moans approach a crescendo.

It is natural for daughters to disdain their mothers, it is a commonplace phenomenon, and sometimes that disdain can reach quite a high volume, Mom knows, Mom remembers how it feels to hold back an orgasm until you cannot, just like Casandra is doing right now, she cannot hold it back and she finishes with a cry, a faint and grating cry Mom can practically feel on the other side of the door like a smack across the face.

"What do you want?" Casandra finally manages to reply. Mom steps back when the door opens: a smell emanates from her daughter and the room, a smell remembered or recognized across the globe, dense like a cloud of moans, one Mom could never forget, not in a thousand years.

Mom could respond with a threat or with some benign question, a comment that would diminish the dramatic effect of Casandra's masturbatory mutiny, her climactic coup d'état, her orgasmic insurrection, her unsubtle expression of contempt toward this woman, whom she considers no more than a breeder, a *Homo sapiens* hen, a vagina with arms and legs. But Mom says nothing. Not immediately. After a beat, she simply replies:

"It's time to eat."

She barely has time to enjoy the look on Cacasandra's face, her hormonal swine eyes eager for another round, ready for another bout in the ring, since the first proved ineffective.

"So hurry up and finish whatever you're doing," Mom adds, "before your father gets home."

Casandra shrugs.

"Okay."

Summer is the worst part of the year, just my opinion. And summer is the only season we get in this country. Forget about spring and fall. Don't even talk to me about winter. Now is the summer of our discontent. A country with only one season, and it's a hot one. That's why people always end up losing their shit here. Look at Dad. That man is the product of a summer that outstayed its welcome. Now all he's got in his head are dreams of retaliation and delusions of grandeur, you can see it, you can smell it. He polishes his medals over and over, thank God they didn't take them from him. Between the heat and a Dad with no vestiges of his former glory to cling to, shit would get real—fast.

Being Casandra has never been easy, okay?

To live here with a name like mine, you have to muster all your patience, take lots of deep breaths, have a purpose in life.

Maybe it's because of the name they gave me, which, for the record, I had no say in whatsoever. Being a Trojan princess in a country like this, with a family like mine, is already an insurmountable task, but with this heat, it's mission impossible.

We spend our days locked inside. Dad says the outside world is crawling with enemies, all the enemies who tried to unhorse him. And succeeded. He's always saying it. So hang in there, Casandra, don't fantasize about the end of summer, because we're on the path of eternal return and that, ladies and gentlemen, is disgusting. Dad is disgusting too, but he doesn't know it. We can't hold it against him. He's disgusting because he barely brushes his teeth and because he loves us too much. There's nothing fouler than a father who loves his kids too much. We are the seeds of evil, but he adores us, he can't live without us.

Blah dee blah. That's the excuse. Super.

So, he doesn't let us go outside. Ever. He's been prepping us for this since we were little. For this scenario and thousands of other potential catastrophes because, as they say, correctly, the higher you climb, the harder you fall, and right now Dad is flailing around in desperate free fall, plummeting with no parachute or protection of any kind, because they popped his hot-air balloon.

Being Casandra has never been easy, okay?

If Mom heard me say that, she'd just write it off. According to her, being Casandra is no harder than being anyone else. That's what she says and that's the end of it, no hesitation or vacillation. Mom considers herself the reservoir of all wisdom, but it's an arid, parched wisdom, good for nothing except feeding the moths. Mom is a little like them, the dusty moths. You can't really hate moths, they serve a purpose, though I still don't have much sense of what Mom's is. Let's be real, she isn't exactly cut out to be the wife of a powerful man, nor is she the very model of a modern maternal ideal, that much is obvious. Being a mom has never been easy, being the wife of a powerful man has never been easy, and being a moth is the hardest of all.

I want to go out, to take a space walk through the neighborhood. Yes, a space walk, I know what I said, I choose my words carefully. Because at this point, strolling through the neighborhood and walking down the same streets we've walked down a million times is an Olympic feat, the Trojan War, a heroic quest akin to conquering outer space because, according to Dad, the eyes of the enemies of the people—that is, the eyes of the enemies of Dad, the man with the medals whom Pop-Pop Mustache has spurned—are a constant threat. And we're the bait.

When I say we, I'm talking about Caleb, Calia, and me, the three saplings, the seeds of evil.

It's about resistance.

It's about patience.

Super.

Dad doesn't understand. You can only ask so much of a man in love with his medals.

It's a relatively short space walk, to be fair, just eight blocks north in a straight line.

There's nothing particularly special about my beloved at first glance. As far as bridges go, she isn't exactly the belle of the barrio; she isn't the cleanest, and she's probably the oldest, and her supports have turned to rust. But you can feel her tenderness pulsing beneath the layers of oxidation, there's no hiding it, no patina of rust could ever conceal her feelings for me. When I touch her, she quivers. Find me a girl who quivers like that when I kiss her. You can't. Find me a girl who'll let me touch her like I touch my beloved, caress her like I caress my beloved. You can't.

I knew my beloved had a feminine essence the first time we did it. I don't care what people say, okay? There's something special about your first time together, something forbidden that fades over time. She has been there all my life—eight blocks, straight north—she's part of the neighborhood, just one bridge of many, so I can't say it was love at first sight, but it was a love of proximity, familiarity, appreciation. That day I touched her and realized she was ready to receive me, so I gave myself to her, rust on skin, steel on bone, and my heart pounded for the two of us until it nearly exploded into orgasm.

Now I'd like to share some thoughts on love and literature.

Shakespeare understood all this way better than I do. Way better than anyone, really, because when Juliet appeared on her balcony, she didn't gaze at Romeo, no; she pressed her body against that chunk of carved rock, pressed her body against it to receive all its love and desire, the ardor of Veronese limestone, more eternal than the affections of any Romeo. With Elizabethan dramaturgy you have to read between the lines, okay? Just read Shakespeare between the lines and you'll see Juliet's passion for the objects of her affection. Don't take my word for it, my name is Casandra and I live in the heat of this endless summer's day, which is neither lovely nor temperate; listen to Shakespeare, he was a much better, prettier writer.

Unlike Juliet, I don't have the object of my affection just through yonder window. She isn't too far, but we're kept a space walk apart by Dad's medals, by paranoia, by Pop-Pop Mustache. Dad spends his days imagining the thousands of forms Pop-Pop Mustache's vengeance might take as I breathe this air so torrid it seems to carry a kiss from my beloved, an iron-oxide kiss begging me to escape, fly, run to her. I know the object of my adoration awaits with a desire more everlasting than any you'd find in fair Verona. And it feels like I'm the heroine, as if I am Juliet, *O happy dagger. This is thy sheath.* The doors of the house are always locked, but the windows—*O happy dagger*—are not. The third-floor windows are an option. Super. One step, another, eaves, careful, jump, *this is thy sheath, there rust*, and I sprint eight blocks straight north without looking back, without a thought for Pop-Pop Mustache, without a thought for anything except the feel of her kiss.

Rust between my lips, rust between my hips, her oxide is my oxygen.

No one who names their children Tunisia and Toronto is normal, regardless of what Caleb thinks. As much as we appreciate his reflections on the ordinary versus the extraordinary, Caleb is still a very young boy, and more importantly, a boy awash in his own problems, which are myriad despite his efforts to conceal them. It is worth noting, too, that Caleb has vaguely erotic feelings for his cousin Tunisia, and he has yet to figure out if he is the victim of a vast conspiracy led by a cabal of terminally ill bunny rabbits and other woebegone creatures, or if he himself is the victimizer, the animal kingdom's royal executioner, sacrilegiously dispatching the lives of nature's most vulnerable citizens. It is important to remember that Caleb does not choose which animals live and which die; the animals make that determination for themselves. This is compelling evidence that a multiplicity of intelligences does in fact exist: any animal familiar with the concept of suicide or euthanasia is worthy of superior-species status, and here we have yet another argument in favor of the environmental cause. We should bear in mind that when a boy like Caleb is faced with the democratic task of imparting death as if it were justice, he does not have very clear notions of right and wrong, of who is normal and who is a freak.

Nevertheless, we must refute the boy, who already has such a troubled mind despite his age. We will not entertain his initial suggestion that his aunt and uncle were normal—which is to say harmless, defenseless, nothing more than a pair of eyeglasses and their attendant poor vision—and therefore could not possibly be enemies of the people or of Caleb's father's medals.

This is more than just a slightly pejorative assessment of the aunt and uncle's peculiar decision to name their children after a country and a city in the world beyond our borders. The mistake lies elsewhere; we will try to explain it as simply as possible. Let us start by stating the obvious: ours is the only country that matters. Everyone knows this, especially those lucky enough to live here, where it is easier to see things for what they are; the outside world is shrouded in darkness, but our own intimate, chaste, interior world is bright, a land where summer reigns supreme, or rather, a land where summer and the General write the laws.

But there are none so blind as those who wish not to see, and Caleb's aunt and uncle—who are also the parents of Tunisia, fifteen years old, and Toronto, eight—willfully chose blindness.

And it is worth asking, what is it that the willfully blind see?

Well, it is as straightforward as it sounds: they see what they want to see and overlook what they would rather ignore. If a willfully blind man searches for stains on the nation, he will find them. Needless to say, the stains are there for a reason; they have been splashed on the fabric of the nation for the willfully blind to discover, a test to reveal who is faithful and who is treacherous. This test is an objective and fair-handed method, as everyone knows, and further reflection on the point is unnecessary because, ultimately, it has little bearing on our story.

Tunisia and Toronto lived as well as anyone could with

those two horrible names and—credit where credit is due—both managed to be relatively normal children. Despite their names, they were not bullied or marginalized at school. In fact, one could describe Tunisia and Toronto as almost popular, unlike Casandra, for example, with her object fetishism, or Caleb and his aforementioned propensity for bumping off bunny rabbits. We only mention the older siblings to avoid broaching a delicate topic: the Calia issue. The family's youngest is a wonderful artist, but that is the best that can be said of her. Compared with those three seeds of evil, Tunisia and Toronto were fairly well assimilated within the adolescent community, that secret society that admits no freaks and immediately exiles excessively freakish individuals from the sculpture garden known as childhood. Moreover, Tunisia and Toronto were so kindhearted that they endeavored to integrate Casandra and Caleb into their social circles at school, yet another point in favor of the bespectacled twosome, who even turned a blind eye to their cousins' continual anomalies, anomalies that came about primarily because Casandra and Caleb were born with a silver spoon in their mouths, which is to say, they were born with medals in their mouths, which these days is tantamount to being royalty.

The root of the problem—credit where credit is due—was not Tunisia and Toronto, who did as well as they could with the names they were assigned at birth, a decision in which they had no say whatsoever. If anything truly freakish can be said of the aunt and uncle's offspring, it is the siblings' singular, shared obsession: geography trivia. Unlike Caleb and Casandra—who barely even knew the names of other countries, as the only name of importance was the sacred name of their homeland—Tunisia and Toronto could locate every city, capital, and state on a map, along with a host of other geographic curiosities, and they were rarely wrong. This geographic mania was subjected to deep analysis in the wake of their parents' political wrongdoing. You have likely inferred the wrongdoing to which we refer, namely the seditious scheme to deliberately put our General Mustache's health in jeopardy, a scheme that we will mention quickly, in passing, and with only the briefest of discussion to avoid setting a bad example for new generations, and especially to avoid planting ideas in said generations' heads with regard to how, why, and when so horrible an event could occur.

The analysis of the aforementioned geography trivia games, at which Tunisia and Toronto were so remarkably proficient, yielded surprising results worthy of examination. We will not conduct that examination here within these pages, of course; we will merely note the suspicious behavior. It is possible that, from an early age, Tunisia and Toronto were raised in the ways of enemies of the people. Their aptitude for locating other countries and cities on a map suggests preparations to flee the country and seek asylum elsewhere. It is difficult to surmise any other reason for Tunisia and Toronto to be so skilled at a game that, at least in this country, has no utility. And with this suspicion noted, we can shift to discussing the matter at hand regarding the aunt-uncle duo, the axis of evil, who ultimately, certainly, must have been the masterminds behind the geography trivia and other, even greater atrocities.

A timeline is necessary in order to comprehensively understand the actions the aunt and uncle undertook in those days preceding the events that concern us.

The uncle liked to eat eggshells—an excellent, natural source of calcium—and the aunt was fond of knitting. Their faces were too similar, as if, with the years, some physical essence had gradually transferred from body to body until they were almost twins. The aunt, for example, did not bear much resemblance to the children's father; that is, she did not look anything like the man with the medals, with whom she shared DNA, and whom one could describe as her own flesh and blood, a bona fide relative in every sense.

There are, of course, numerous photos of the aunt and Dad when they were youths. Together on the beach, kneeling, looking at the camera with the surprise of children who merely wish to play in the sand without stopping to satisfy some grown-up whim, namely that of documenting everything that ever happens with a photo; there is poetic irony, we admit, that Dad inherited that very same custom of photographing every aspect of his family's life.

We must also confess that after Dad learned of the duo's incriminating actions and General Mustache summoned him to his office—that is, to the table of regret—he burned almost all photos of his childhood in a vain attempt to divest himself of those memories in which his sister was present. This proved useless because General Mustache was concerned not with the burned photos but with the knowledge that one of his right-hand men was a relative—no, a full-fledged biological brother—of an enemy of the people, and not just any enemy of the people, but an enemy of the people of the very worst order. Dad was brother to an antidemocrat, to a willfully blind, bomb-planting terrorist who attempted to assassinate the General, which is another way of saying she attempted to assassinate the nation.

And here the time line helps us understand events.

The aunt and uncle were the bombmakers. First, they sent Tunisia and Toronto to their paternal grandparents' house; they said their goodbyes with a guilty expression, but the die was cast, *alea jacta est*; if the General died, Tunisia and Toronto's parents would return as heroes, but if the General survived, *alea jacta est*, Tunisia and Toronto would be the children of anti-patriots, enemies of the people, blood on their hands.

The explosive was homemade, but very effective.

The identities of the duo's coconspirators remain unclear. They were no doubt colluding with someone in a position of power, hence why Dad found his neck locked in a pillory of distrust. In order to reach the General, one must be close to the General, and Dad would have made as good a rat, as good a contact as anyone, although the evidence thus far suggests the contrary. That is, even though Dad appears fairly innocent and the duo had other seditious and antidemocratic relationships, Dad remains under suspicion.

The aunt and uncle's coconspirators transported the bomb.

The aunt and uncle only built it.

General Mustache is no fool. Those who think so are the true fools.

The bomb never went off. It was intercepted by military intelligence.

Shock and horror, a homemade explosive was nearly placed beneath the platform from which General Mustache would extemporize one of his famous speeches.

Explosive disabled.

Problem nearly resolved.

Ah, no, wait . . .

There are some who say the uncle was in the audience,

among those gathered to hear the speech, and he was armed with a handgun.

There are some who say the uncle wanted to know if the General's heart had a mustache too.

Not much has been said about the aunt. At the time she had been knitting a scarf that no one would ever use, at least not in this country, further proof of the duo's plans to flee to a land where winter is less than a pipe dream.

The uncle was arrested with the weapon on his person. The aunt was arrested after she made the final stitch of her scarf.

Thirty years in prison: four short words that represent the average life expectancy of a human being in the Middle Ages, give or take a few years.

We have learned nothing of Tunisia and Toronto. We have no need. They live with their paternal grandparents, and they lead dejected, joyless lives. As the progeny of two would-be assassins, they have naturally been shunned by this nation's definitively normal adolescent population. There is no room on the playground for the offspring of two willfully blind terrorists who looked so hard for stains on the nation they ended up finding them.

Alea jacta est.

As this is not the story of Tunisia and Toronto, we will no longer discuss them or their parents, but rather the fate of Dad.

Dad's fate is cause for concern.

It is not paranoia.

General Mustache is no friend to would-be traitors and Dad has won the lottery, the abject lottery of association and doubt.

In the eyes of the world, Dad is no longer to be trusted.

This is no time for drama. You can smell it. Cacasandra is nowhere to be found and the house is a cauldron of nerves. Mom tries to conceal a smile, hoping no one notices her relief. With the firstborn absent, it is easier for her to mask the contempt she feels for Calia, who is working on her drawing, apathetic to what is happening around her as Dad howls and stutters the missing girl's name, getting lost in idiot conspiracies about the family getting whisked off at night, drowned in a dark well, and now his Cacasandra, his virginal teenage Cacasandra may well be the next victim in a nation that is coming apart at the seams. Needless to say, in this context we are not talking about the nation as a physical place or as a political blast furnace—or if we are, we are doing it in a symbolic sense—we are talking about the collapse of the nation in Dad's heart. Now there is no turning back: formerly justified acts have been revealed for what they were, it is not the same when other people's children are the ones in jeopardy or in the political crosshairs; those individuals back then were terrorists, enemies of the people. Dad would bite his tongue and suppress this sort of idea if he had the strength, but there is no time, how could there be time if Cacasandra is nowhere to be found.

Mom's surreptitious smiling continues and Dad looks at her uneasily, what does this woman have to smile about, the danger is palpable, smellable, the house is seething with dread, and we should add for effect that even Caleb appears apathetic. Dad feels a twinge of trepidation, there is something he does not know, something the others are hiding from him, a domestic drama behind curtains that, until this moment, have been closed to him. No one is thinking about Cacasandra, no one is thinking about Dad, who has retreated to the drawer where he hides his precious medals. He placed them there as a gesture of political prudence; it is better not to wear them on his chest, even though that is where they belong, pinned to the uniform he has continued to wear every day even after his fall from grace, because a soldier always does his duty, or at least dons duty's lost laurels. But the medals have a propensity to rust in the drawer, and eternal vigilance is the price of lustrous medals. Take care of your medals, do not let them rust, make sure they get lots of fresh air, one day they will be back in their rightful place, on your chest, after General Mustache realizes that this has all been a big misunderstanding, that you have been wronged, that a hero is yearning for his honor to be restored. For now, the medals have their place and Dad airs them daily, polishes them, has crafted a new routine to ward off the bad habit of waiting for time to pass.

But today is a special day, a potentially tragic day, though the smile on Mom's face would suggest anything but. Where is Cacasandra, Dad inquires, and the others shrug. It is in the air, that smell, that secret bubbling away in a cruel cauldron, and Dad feels like an idiot, feels a world away from his own flesh and blood, he has become a stranger in his own home. But this is no time for that sort of thinking. This is no time for self-pity. Dad opens the drawer and selects the most illustrious medals, pins them to the uniform, straightens them on his chest; haste and distress may make him stutter, but they don't strip him of

ELAINE VILAR MADRUGA

his hero's decorum, so he stands for the requisite time before the mirror.

Mom's face scrutinizes him. Mom's face peers over one of the uniform sleeves.

"Why are you so upset? It's nothing to worry about. She's young."

Dad clicks his tongue. His wife's superficial tone irks him. That tone confirms that nothing is happening aside from the secret that is well-known among the rest of his family. No need to tell Dad what this is all about; Dad is a foreigner between the walls of his own home.

"Whewhewhere is Cacasandra?"

His voice conveys danger, speaks to his fears, and Mom stops smiling. For a long time now, the man with the medals has been a visitor, a tourist of his family's dynamics. He knows little about Casandra, less about Caleb, and nothing about Calia, though he cannot be faulted for the last; there is no telling what is in Calia's head, butterflies or elephants, death or life.

Mom is not so hard-hearted. She is, in fact—still—capable of pity. Not for her children. In her ledger of feelings and emotional states, they are in a separate column. But she reacts with compassion when she gazes upon the man and his medals, lost and drowning in guilt.

"She's okay. She's young," she repeats, and in the woman's voice Dad hears a sardonic tone, though he would be hard-pressed to say if it was one of mockery or retribution. "Kids need a little freedom to do the things they want."

"What things?"

He is a patient man. Undoubtedly. He cannot violate the rules he himself set for the household, but sometimes it is difficult, sometimes it is nearly impossible not to raise his voice, not to impose military discipline in this domestic barracks chock-full of slovenly soldiers: an unconcerned mother, an insubordinate daughter, an indifferent son, and Calia, indescribable by any word other than her own name. Naturally, a certain degree of imprudence is expected from the children. Mom is half correct about youth, which makes children so unthinking they'll walk bright-eyed and oblivious into a minefield. Dad is angry at the mother, at the woman tasked with looking after the children. How hard can it be to raise them? The children are the way they are because Mom either cannot understand or cannot smell the danger. Only a week ago, they withdrew surveillance from the house. Only a few months ago, the aunt and uncle became enemies of the people. One false step could bring even greater disgrace upon the family. Dad already explained all of this with a wealth of detail. He stressed the urgency of remaining indoors, noted that a wasted summer was nothing in a lifetime of summers and, at that time, they all agreed. They did not care about the time they would lose locked inside the house, a house besieged by General Mustache's eyes and ears.

"Don't worry, don't waste your time," Mom sighs, sitting on the edge of the bed and brushing her hair with both hands. "Casandra will be back. She's . . ."

"What? What is she?" Dad has forgotten to stutter, and the medals are arranged perfectly on his uniform.

"She's in love," Mom says, before adding, "She's young. Isn't youth disgusting?"

There are no lies in the woman's voice. Her mouth has twisted into another strange smile.

H ow old are you, Casandra?"

"Seriously?"

"I asked how old you are. It's part of the protocol."

"Dumb fucking protocol."

"Why do you say that?"

"Because you know I'm sixteen."

"Very good, we're making a little progress. See how easy it is . . . ? Sixteen."

"Whatever. Dumb. Fa-la-la."

"What is it that you consider 'dumb'?"

"I already told you."

"That I asked your age? Why?"

"Didn't you give birth to me?"

"Well, we have to follow the protocol, and it's part of the protocol."

"Dumb fucking protocol."

"You have already expressed that point of view."

"You aren't my therapist. You're my mother."

"Then why don't you ever call me Mom outside of our sessions?"

". . . dunno. Don't want to, I guess."

"Or perhaps it's because you don't love me."

"Oh, yeah. That too, I guess."

"Do you want to talk about your relationship with your mother?"

"You're fucked in the head."

"Why do you think that? Does it strike you as impersonal that I refer to your mother in the third person?"

"Literally so fucked."

"Enacting violence through language won't make you feel any better about your condition."

"Blah dee blah. I'm not sick."

"We could talk about your, you know . . ."

"About my what?"

". . . your attractions."

"You can say it better than that, try."

"What do you mean?"

"Saying 'your attractions' is super impersonal, okay?"

"How would you prefer I refer to them?"

"Dunno. Improvise."

"That's something we can address in therapy later on."

"Dumb fucking therapy."

"I appreciate your honesty. I appreciate that you freely express your point of view. That's part of growing up."

"Definitely, totally, I agree with you one hundred percent."

"What did we say about irony, Casandra?"

"'Irony is not a suitable tool for dialogue.' Whatever, I still think that's dumb. Irony is the most important condiment in any conversation between thinking creatures."

"It's wonderful how we can have such differing points of view, don't you think?"

"I think you wouldn't be interested in knowing my point of view about you."

"We're in therapy to talk about you, Casandra, not me."

"Okay. Your loss. It would be very helpful for you."

"So, your attractions—"

"Again with the 'your attractions'!"

"It's a generalization that will facilitate both of us channeling this dialogue toward your erotic interest in objects . . . now, tell me, are you not attracted to human beings?"

"No."

"Why is that?"

"Another dumb fucking question."

"Why is that?"

"Humans don't smell like iron oxide."

"That's a good point. Are you talking about your . . . affinity . . . ?"

"The word is 'relationship.'"

"A relationship is a bond between two people, Casandra. Something inanimate cannot offer any sort of bond."

"According to you. What do you know? I've never seen anything more inanimate than Dad. And you still slept with him, didn't you? That's how you ended up with the three of us, Cacasandra, Cacaleb, and Cacalia."

"We aren't here to talk about my relationship with your father. We're here to discuss your relationship with objects."

"At least you said relationship. I'm curious: Is Dad good in bed? Doesn't seem like it. I've always wondered."

"We aren't here to talk about your father and his sexual prowess or lack thereof."

"Blah blah blah, whatever. Have you even had an orgasm? At least one? Did he ever make you come? Or if you wanted to feel anything, did you have to work for it yourself? Dad's not exactly the kind of man who'd go—"

"Down to business now, Casandra, we are here to talk about you. We aren't here to talk about my life, period."

"So, no. He didn't do anything for you. Must've been pretty boring. I can't believe the three of us made it into this world. See? And you call that a 'relationship.'"

"Your conflict-avoidance mechanisms are quite interesting, Casandra."

"Yeah I know, blah blah conflict, blah blah mechanism, blah blah Casandra, fa-la-la-la-la."

"For how long have you felt attracted to . . ."

"To what?"

"Don't make this difficult."

"You're the therapist."

"What did we say about irony?"

"It's a condiment."

"How about we do a quick evaluation."

"Oh, please no, the ink blots again? I'm not a freak."

"What makes you think you would be?"

"The way you look at me. What right do you have to look at me like that? Stop it, okay? If I'm a freak, what the fuck does that make you?"

"I'd like to know what makes you feel as if I am judging you."

"It's what you do best."

"That isn't true, Casandra. I'm here to help you. You can't use generalizations and feelings to co-opt this dialogue."

"You're here because you hate me. And because you're trying to love me, but it's not going so good, right? Don't worry. I don't mind. Caleb doesn't either. I dunno about Calia, but I think she cares more about the butts on her monkeys than kisses from her mommy. How does it make you feel that one of your daughters thinks monkey butts are more important than her own mother?"

"Shut up."

"How about we do a quick evaluation. Answer the following question: In what year did you most recently experience the physiological phenomenon known as an orgasm?"

"I won't allow you to co-opt this dialogue, Casandra."

"You have a husband who'd rather finger his medals than sleep with you. The fact that the three of us were ever born is a miracle. Should we talk about that? On the day we were conceived, did you have to dress up as Pop-Pop Mustache?"

"You're a spoiled little shit. This session is over."

"Okay, whatever you say. Your loss, Mom. I think discussing these issues could be very helpful for you. You clearly need it."

"I said the session is over."

"Okay. I'll be around if you need me. Should I tell Caleb to come in?"

Now our death begins," the aunt said, to which everyone in the house reacted with applause.

Her voice was a fissure; there was something unnatural in the way the words flowed from her mouth, catching between her teeth. Even so, kid-Mom remembered those syllables' effect, the miracle by which the woman without a voice suddenly found one, and value added, through it came the voice of God. Kid-Mom thought God's voice was a little too sharp and raw, the sound of a mangy cat. Such an ugly voice for so great a god, and such peculiar first words for the formerly silent aunt, who was now an interpreter of the heavens, an emissary from that remote place where the divine resided.

"Now our death begins."

Nor had kid-Mom forgotten the butterflies and their bright wings. From that moment on, butterflies allied themselves to the cause of the family's disappearance, of their mass extinction. Kid-Mom recalled how the aunt, God's mouthpiece, had approached her, caressed her forehead.

"Not yours," she said in her mangy stray-cat voice.

The aunt's eyes burned with light from another world, and kid-Mom felt a consuming fear that encompassed not just that woman's presence but all the air she breathed, which was filled with omens and portents of impending death. Just then, kid-Mom was struck with the certainty that her aunt's voice had changed her forever, made her different. Why or for what purpose, she could not know, and she would not know until much later, until Calia was born with the aunt's eyes, yes, the eyes of the silent aunt who had vanished long ago.

Calia was born in the winter, which is to say, at the time of year when the calendar stipulates that the unrelenting heat ought to relent, a prophecy all hoped would be fulfilled soon, a promise that renewed at the close of every three-hundred-and-sixty-five-day cycle, three-hundred and sixty-six on leap years. Calia was born in a pandemic of dire heat that seemed to spite the calendar.

It's summer now, summer then, summer always in this piece of shit country, Mom said to herself as she pushed hard and sweated harder, the placenta coming out through her pores instead of between her legs; it seemed as if blood were trickling down her forehead. It's summer now, summer then, summer always in this disgusting country, Mom said to herself, squeezing her legs, squeezing her mind, and at that instant, Calia came into the world, on the hottest day recorded that year.

That seemed like an omen from hell and maybe it was. It is important to avoid commenting on matters that cannot be proven one way or the other. What is certain is that when Mom held Calia in her arms, the baby opened her eyes. That is not odd in and of itself; there are precocious children, alert children, but something else weighed heavy in that gaze, something different, a memory perhaps. Mom knew it immediately and did not have to turn the cogs of her recollection back far, did not have to grease them: newborn Calia's eyes were identical to the aunt's, the same dead radiance, the same certainty of having entered the world as God's mouthpiece to herald in the hour of our death. No heat can impede the will of the divine. The first time Calia cried, Mom recognized the meow of that cat, that same mangy cat that was God, surely those sounds were not words, surely they were just cries for breasts and milk, a cry for refuge, but Mom threw the girl to the foot of the bed and felt alone, tremendously alone and not understood by the world.

"Not yours," the aunt had said, years earlier when Mom was just a child. "Yours later."

Mom remembered those words.

Later had arrived and Calia was there to remind her that someday—someday soon—her time would come.

God meowed one more time in Calia's cries, and then the girl fell silent.

I run the eight blocks that separate me from my beloved. Some turn their heads. Some think they recognize me. The neighbors point. They know who I am. Meaning they know who Dad is, or who Dad *was*. It's like my identity and my name are a sign I drag around above my head. I'm like a character in a comic book with a speech balloon floating beside me. The speech balloon acts as a signal, a reflection of my status within a family marred by Dad's story.

The tedious sun and eight blocks are endless, so I run faster, get winded, regret it, regret not doing aerobics, regret not exercising on the school playground—if I had, I'd be able to reach my beloved without pausing to catch my breath. I stop, and in some ways, it's fun to see how, on the sly, the neighbors try to steer clear of me. Greetings, fellow patriots! It's me, the bubonic plague, the black death. I even wave to a few, who then look at their feet; I am my father's daughter and the nation pretends not to know me.

If at least the neighbors had the decency to not look at me, if they lowered their heads immediately, my criticism would be more constructive, okay? All of humanity would still be totally chickenshit, but at least it wouldn't also be a sack of shit.

I try to quicken my pace and, to be obnoxious, to make sure they know who I am, I say hello to everyone I see. I don't just wave or make small gestures of familiarity, your garden-variety,

Hey, how's it going. No, no, I trot over with arms outstretched like these pedestrians are my long-lost relatives, or I get creative, I call out, *See you this afternoon, It was so fun hanging out yesterday, Come back and see us again soon, We missed you, You're my very best friend.* Obviously, these childish comments demonstrate my childish vendetta. They induce widespread panic, make eyes open wide until they protrude from their sockets, and obviously, everyone runs, makes the fastest getaway they can, glancing over their shoulders as if Pop-Pop Mustache himself were lurking down the street, taking down names, addresses, and relationships based on my public effusions of affection.

Yeah, yeah I know, fear is loneliness in its purest form, but I don't feel like waxing philosophical right now, okay? Because my inducement to escape the house—that is, the cage Dad built for us—is a sublime and vulgar act, the desire to be united with my beloved, to straddle her and feel the oxidized undulations of her architecture, for her to feel the protuberances of my anatomy.

On the last block, I stop running. I'd rather make myself presentable. I see her in the distance and immediately I'm wet. She's there, and I'm wet. I smell her, her vibrations reverberating through the air; I know she recognizes me, that she's impatient to see me, which only heightens my arousal. I approach her, caress her, and yes, beneath my hand, I feel her tremble; she wants me, she needs me, now is the moment to lift my dress—thank God it's a dress and not something that would hamper our union—I pull down my thong, climb atop a piece of her structure, and my beloved purrs for me. She likes me on top, gyrating, rust inside of me, and it doesn't matter if anyone's watching, if they even care, okay? It doesn't matter, it doesn't even matter a few minutes later when Dad's hand grabs me by the shoulder, tears me away from her structure and away from my pleasure.

Goodbye, my love, goodbye, like Juliet I return to confinement and Dad clearly knows he's playing the role of Juliet's nurse. His hand is rigid, I struggle against it, I want to break free, rust inside of me, goodbye, my love, goodbye, my love, I cry out, and Dad lifts a hand, now I'll finally get it, here comes the violence he's never dared give me, it's time, but he only picks up my underwear, pulls down my dress, Dad doesn't cry, men don't cry, but he drags me by the arm, shielding me from curious eyes.

He thinks it's a particular way of protecting me.

Fear in the eyes of others is loneliness in its most distilled form.

CALEB

Caleb sat on the front patio banister. That banister had been the outer border of his universe ever since Dad canceled summer and prohibited all contact with the outside world. Now the universe was sliced in two: In the first slice—Dad's sealed-off enclosure, the house they were obliged to share, a place that never used to seem quite so tight or claustrophobic—paranoia reigned supreme; the second slice was the realm of danger, though that danger was not always visible on the surface, was not always self-evident. Sometimes it existed only in the pronouncements of his father, who took daily pains to scour for tracking devices, bugs, tapped phones, hidden cameras in the house's thousand dark corners. Caleb yawned and, for a moment, remembered Tunisia's thick eyeglasses, her freckle-speckled nose. The boredom of that locked-down summer was worse than the nation's inexhaustible heat.

"Cacaleb, go inside and close the windows!" Dad commanded as he stormed out of the house to search for Casandra. Then he whispered, with an almost disappearing voice, "And watch out for those anants, Cacaleb, they're cocoming for you."

And it was true. A small battalion of ants had begun to scale the patio stairs, marching toward the young messenger of death's legs.

"Stay with Cacalia, don't open the door. That's an order. Get inside. Dodon't let them see you."

Dad's wild eyes contrasted with his calm voice, the voice of a soldier accustomed to ordering troops to hold together in disaster scenarios by any means necessary. Caleb pulled up his legs. Moved away from the ants. Obeyed.

He wished Casandra would leave for good.

He silently hoped Dad's most horrific fears would come true. The house's suffocating paranoia must have had a specific purpose, a particular bull's-eye Dad was hoping to hit, but his marksmanship was suspect.

He wished Casandra would disappear once and for all.

Caleb chewed his lip and picked up a dead sparrow. Everyone knew sparrow hearts were sensitive, and the summer heat was not doing them any favors. Maybe it had fallen dead in the garden all on its own. Or maybe not. Maybe the sparrow had brushed the boy's head, maybe it was another one of the suicidal birds that assailed Caleb from all sides, seeking the sweet relief of death, nosediving like kamikazes to fulfill some divine purpose Caleb did not understand. It did not matter now anyway; the sparrow was broken and its scant utility was to form part of the young angel of death's collection, his collection of still lifes.

He had begun to collect dead animals a year earlier, at the advice of his therapist-mother. She would purse her lips whenever she spoke to Caleb in her improvised office, a repurposed bedroom.

"You'll have to do something with the bodies," she had said. "I'm referring to the large and medium-size animals, Caleb. Forget about the insects. Who's going to notice something so small? They practically vanish. But it would be a terrible waste to deprive the other creatures of a purpose. In nature, everything has a purpose. In nature, everything is recycled."

Mom was right, and although it took some time, Caleb eventually put her advice into practice. After a few months, he had discovered his own true calling in life.

Art.

Or something like it.

An installation of dead birds, squirrels, rabbits, a stray cat, some toads, a couple of snakes: a monument to the uncertainty of life and the steady spiral of decay, an ever-evolving work whose progress depended on a steady stream of suicidal animals and Caleb's willingness to play angel of mercy.

Art hidden in the basement.

A living jigsaw of dead pieces.

Only Casandra had seen this work of installation art once, by accident. She had been searching for an old camera lens—Dad usually kept his obsolete photography equipment next to a dusty trunk of old photos, since there was no good place to keep it except in that dank basement—when, instead, she discovered Caleb's puzzle of rotting flesh and yellowing bones.

Casandra was cold-blooded. As cold-blooded as a mutant chicken. She went upstairs to Caleb's room and entered without knocking.

"You're disgusting, okay? Bunnykiller Caleb."

Caleb looked up, squeezed a particularly bothersome pimple on his forehead, and replied:

"Well, you're a pervert."

There was no need to say more. Each sibling understood what the other was referring to under the seams. Casandra glared at him with contempt.

"You'll never get a girlfriend. You're gonna die a virgin,

okay? Bunnykillers always die virgins. There isn't a girl any-where in the world who'd let a bunnykiller like you stick it in."

Caleb shrugged.

"If you keep killing bunny rabbits, I'm gonna . . ." Casandra tried to improvise a threat, but it ended up hanging in the thresh-old of her mouth.

"You're gonna what? Tell Mom? Dad? Calia?" He almost choked on his laughter.

It was an absurd threat. Mom was the one who came up with the idea of repurposing death as art, Dad did not care about anything but his medals, and Calia lived in a world of paint-brushes and pencil drawings where nothing existed except ana-tomically correct monkey butts.

"I'll tell Tunisia."

The cousin's name rang in Caleb's mind. It felt like an an-eurysm, like a bulging, weakened area in the middle of his head that could burst at any moment. Worse was the stabbing sensa-tion in his heart. Tunisia, fifteen years old with oversize eye-glasses. Caleb was nauseous. He became so nervous he even began to stutter a little—maybe it was a genetic trait.

"Don't even thithink about it."

Casandra smiled derisively.

"Cousinfucker," she said. "Bunnykiller."

Even though all this transpired early in the year of family disgrace, Caleb could not forget Casandra's threat.

Having and hating an older sister might seem redundant, but hatred was exactly what Caleb felt toward the girl to whom he was bound through microscopic skeins of DNA. That is why, weeks later, he had to hold back his laughter when he saw her staggering back down the street. Dad was dragging her by the arm; neither said a word. It was a picturesque scene, at least to Caleb, who watched from the patio banister, taking in the tableau of his dethroned sister. Dad's medals jostled on his chest. They sounded like tin. Caleb surreptitiously picked up the dead sparrow and, with no small effort, managed to cram it into one of his jeans pockets.

"Cacasandra, go to your room," Dad said in the doorway.

"What happened?" Caleb asked, struggling not to laugh.

Dad shrugged.

"Nothing, Cacaleb. Go inside the house. Shut the dodoor! Didn't I already tell you? Why does nono one ever obey my orders?"

Silently, Caleb crossed the threshold.

"Sparrowkiller," Casandra whispered when her younger brother stepped into the front hall.

"Bridgefucker," Caleb replied.

The aunt, once silent but now speaking, was not the one who decided the mode of death that best suited the family dynamic. For days, her guttural mangy-cat voice gave precise instructions, and everyone listened, immersed in an ecstasy of adoration that kid-Mom observed from her hiding place in the next room. They weighed various methods and their relative difficulty. Someone suggested maybe God would like it if they cut their veins open, since it would remind him of the olden days, those magnificent times of yesteryear when he was constantly lavished with myrrh, gold, and sacrificed doves, but the aunt responded with a dissatisfied smile, indicating that, based on the directives she had received from on high, this would be a suboptimal approach. Then she returned to her butterflies and gave no further instruction. It was kid-Mom's grandmother who made the decision, resolving that poison offered a hygienic compromise, a solution God would certainly appreciate, and one that would not require them to repurpose and suffer under the blade of the family's butcher knife.

"God will understand," the old lady said, gazing at her daughter, who continued to draw butterflies that every day grew larger, more colorful, and less lifelike. Just to be sure—since God's will was inscrutable to all except this once-silent, now-speaking drawer of butterflies—kid-Mom's grandmother asked her daughter for confirmation: "Right, honey?"

Kid-Mom's aunt assented with a smile that the family thought was perfect. Through that smile, God communicated with the worshipful, prostrate human race, with the final witnesses who would be right there, kneeling before the sketched butterflies, to commune and adore him forever in their world without end, which is to say, during the days on earth they had left.

They seasoned their meal with poison, like any other ingredient. In fact, the family allowed themselves an act of gluttony, the best possible farewell to the real world: they cooked meat and fish topped with massive servings of rodenticide. The repast included all manner of traditional sweets: flan, rice pudding, cheesecake, as well as fruit juice, papaya, melon, guanabana, immense pots of rice, and tamales. They would die in lavish abundance and enter paradise well-fed, like butterflies too fat to fly, who nevertheless, thanks to the hand of God, would flee this sterile promontory and ascend to the wondrous dimension. The family went about making the merry preparations for their suicide. Kid-Mom, too, was to attend the feast. For her, they cooked a separate, nonlethal dinner. The aunt and God's orders were specific: the girl had to live, for she would bring the divine seed back into the world.

The banquet was a triumph, a celebration of death at which the whole family gathered. They blasted music, danced to exhaustion, and played dominoes and other board games that extracted cries of victory. Kid-Mom's aunt was the perfect hostess. She embraced all the dinner guests, served dish after dish, brought around a tray of juices. For once in her life, she forgot about her butterfly drawings.

Kid-Mom was told to eat the plate set aside for her, and the hostess-aunt was affectionate with her, even giving her a kiss on the cheek. A kiss that felt like a bite. One by one, family members began to fall ill. First, it was nausea and stomach pains, which could have been mistaken for any other malaise except they seemed only to escalate in severity. It was then that the aunt picked up kid-Mom, carried her to an empty bedroom, and said:

"Wait here until you don't hear anything." The mangy tone of her voice contrasted with the fragrance of her mouth, redolent of jasmine and fruit pulp.

The aunt kissed her again on the cheek, another kiss that was practically a bite.

"Goodbye. We'll see each other again soon," the aunt said before closing the door.

On the other side, the first cries and sobs were beginning. Kid-Mom sat very still, as her aunt had instructed, so as not to incur God's wrath by fidgeting, sneezing, or going for help. Slowly, she put an ear against the bedroom door. She was in the room where her aunt slept, where the walls were papered over in hundreds, thousands of butterfly drawings.

When it was finally quiet outside, when the sound of retching had abated and the vomit had ceased to flow like metaphorical manna from heaven in the form of literal digestive waste, when the death rattles of the now permanently silent aunt stopped sounding, kid-Mom knew she could leave the room. But she stayed there. She could not bring herself to open the door.

Above her, atop the walls, perched on the ground, and wherever her gaze landed, there were butterflies, alive, no longer anatomically perfect, but real-world creatures. Kid-Mom tried not to squash the insects as she walked, but the room was teeming with them, and a dozen or so ended up pulverized beneath her feet.

They fluttered in desperation. The butterflies did not want to die, but kid-Mom loathed them. She loathed them because she knew those insects were alive and that in that grown-up world of death behind the door, nothing awaited her except loneliness. So, she crushed more. With rage, with relish. With an assassin's smile. And for the first time, kid-Mom was happy. Slaughtering butterflies, it turns out, had been the key to her happiness all along.

op-Pop Mustache's lap is comfortable. Casandra is too old for dolls now, but Pop-Pop Mustache still shows up every week with a package wrapped in pink paper.

"Open it, open it!" he urges her, and she smiles, feigns joy, feigns surprise, feigns she positively cannot take it any longer, feigns she cannot possibly handle seeing such a tidily wrapped pink box. She tears off the bow, rips at the paper, and feigns adoration as she embraces her new doll.

Casandra is too old to sit on Pop-Pop Mustache's lap, but he insists:

"Come, come . . . tell your old Pop-Pop something he doesn't know."

Casandra fabricates elaborate realities, imaginary adventures, fictional dispatches from childhood, to which Pop-Pop Mustache listens with boyish delight. He does not seem to notice how Casandra has grown, how she wears the same ruffled dress every week so that, when he looks at her, he sees the same little girl she once was. Casandra knows that ignorance is also power, so for as long as Pop-Pop Mustache wants to imagine she is eight years old, she will play along.

"You never talk about your father, Casandrita. Is he good to you?" Pop-Pop Mustache asks, seemingly out of the blue, without conferring importance on his words or allowing the slightest emotion to mar his face, but Casandra is not an idiot, she can smell danger.

"Daddy works a lot . . . ," she says, deploying her best girlish smile, the one that raises dimples on her cheeks, the one that usually makes Pop-Pop Mustache cower with tenderness. But today it achieves nothing.

Pop-Pop Mustache pulls a cigarette from his military jacket and lights it.

Casandra coughs. That is what a little girl is supposed to do in the presence of smoking grown-ups.

"You're big enough now to handle your Pop-Pop smoking around you, right, Casandrita?" And the instant he says this, Casandra notices, for the first time, the penetrating gaze of a man who does not wear medals, who does not need them; it is he who bestows medals and he who takes them away.

"Uh-huh." She decides not to lie.

"So let's talk about your father."

"He's good to me."

". . . but he doesn't give you dolls. He must not have much time for that sort of thing, right?"

"I guess."

"So what does your father spend his time doing?"

"I dunno."

"Sure, sure, you may not know . . . but you're a big girl now, you see and hear everything that goes on in this house. For example, what do you think of your aunt and uncle?"

"My aunt and uncle?"

"Your aunt and uncle gave their children such peculiar names, don't you think? Tunisia and Toronto. What a disservice they did their children with those horrible names. Such a strange choice for these times, and this country."

"Yeah." Casandra decides to be friendly so Pop-Pop Mustache will not get mad. "Caleb is in love with Tunisia."

"Really?"

"Uh-huh."

"And how does your father get along with Tunisia's parents? Do they talk much? Visit a lot?"

"I mean . . . I guess so."

"Of course they do, they're family, it's normal for them to talk. But do they ever talk about me, Casandrita?"

Casandra feels Pop-Pop Mustache's cigarette smoke filtering into her brain. It is dense like fog.

"Maybe. I dunno. I guess."

"Now, Casandrita, don't be shy. You must have heard something. The walls have ears. Don't you know the walls always tell me things?" For an instant, Pop-Pop Mustache smiles like he used to, almost tenderly, but without familiarity. "Your father is an important man. Are you proud of him?"

"I guess."

"Of course you are. What does your father say about me? Does he talk about your Pop-Pop?"

"He says you're tall."

"He says more than that. You're a very smart girl . . . a very smart young woman, Casandra. And smart young women hear much more than they let on. But you know it's bad to hide things from your old Pop-Pop, don't you?"

Yes, Casandra knew this well. It does not take much for a Pop-Pop to shape-shift into a General.

"He's scared," Casandra finally whispers, then adds, in case she was not explicit enough, "of you."

"That must be where you get that big brain of yours from, Casandrita. Your father is right to be afraid of Pop-Pop Mustache. Now, tell me, what do your aunt and uncle say? When they meet with your father?"

"I dunno. They talk alone. On the patio. Outside. Or other places."

"What other places?"

"I dunno. Out somewhere."

"It would make your old Pop-Pop Mustache very happy if his Casandrita would tell the truth."

Puff of smoke. Right in Casandra's face. Cough.

"You know what I've always believed? A stutterer never says the wrong thing." Pop-Pop Mustache's smile looks like a mask. "Don't you think? Speaking so slowly . . . repeating all those syllables . . . it gives a man a lot of time to think. That's why I always say you can't trust a man who stutters."

Puff of smoke. Cough.

"You're getting too old for dolls, Casandra. You're growing up. Next time I'll pick out something better. Like a dress. Would you like one of those nice dresses all the girls your age want? With a nice floral design?"

Puff of smoke.

"Tunisia and Toronto, what heinous names! Although, now that I think about it, Casandra isn't such a common name either. Neither is Caleb, or Calia. The names people give their children speak volumes. We are what we name, Casandrita. Do you know what an ideological problem is? It isn't just a problem with an individual's conscience, but with the conscience of a nation. For example, a name like Casandra might suggest a certain deviation in one's way of thinking," Pop-Pop Mustache crushed the end of his cigarette against the chair's wooden surface. "Don't you think?"

Casandra nodded in silence. She did not know what else to do.

"All right. Now, tell me about your father. Don't worry. You can be honest with your Pop-Pop Mustache. And if you're a good girl, Casandrita, next time I'll bring you a pretty floral dress, the kind big girls wear. Okay?"

The man is shouting, and every cry wraps around the hooves of the elephant that totters on the page. Floats in on a current that melts into the hairs on the trunk. Calia listens to the clinking of the medals, a sound so quiet only she can hear it. There are many sounds like that. For example, the man's blood throbs strangely through his aorta. It is easy to identify the pulsations in the man-with-the-medals' aorta, and even easier to hear the grating of rust between the girl in the floral dress's inner thigh. And why can no one else hear the sound of fingernails against skin, Calia wonders, or the sound of slow-spreading eczema somewhere outside and far from the house, all the cracklings and convulsions of a cacophonous world. Calia presses her pencil against the white sheet so it crunches, only to suddenly encounter the eyes of the woman.

"Calia, look at me."

Calia does not obey. More important are the color and sound of the wing that has begun to emerge from the elephant, between two hooves.

"I said look at me. We have to talk."

Looking up would not be difficult. But it is not a priority. She must determine how she will trace the curvature of the elephant wing, which is undergoing a process of transfiguration, becoming a cocoon. In the artist's mind, an anatomically perfect beast can become a winged mutant.

"It's you, isn't it?" asks the woman in the high-heel shoes, whom Calia knows by a specific name, one syllable, a voiced consonant split by a long vowel: *mm-ah-mm*.

Why would the woman's wishes matter?

Hoof and wing.

Hoof becoming wing.

Butterfly is elephant's sleep pod.

Elephant as protobutterfly.

Calia listens closely; the woman staring at her is an aggregation of indiscernible sounds only Calia can detect. It is difficult to focus on the drawing when the woman's hair keeps crunching. Add up all the crunching, and you will realize no creature's hair ever stops growing, not even in death; hair is our only living companion, the only thing that demonstrates how the thrust of life eclipses the thrust of extinction; we are not as finite as they want us to think; everywhere the world is teeming with silent sounds. For example, in the infrasonic category, the flies' larvae are growing all around, and the flies themselves emit microexplosions every time they shit on the curtains that shield the windows from the eyes of inquisitive passersby. In fact, at this exact instant, just as Calia is attempting to focus all her logic on the drawing, a fly has decided to land and shit upon one of the medals clinking on the man's chest. The plop of fly shit on yellowish tin that has been inaccurately designated a *gold alloy* is the only beautiful thing, the only tolerable thing Calia manages to absorb. Then, once again, she hears the woman's voice:

"I just want you to tell me the truth. Tell me if it's you, if you're in there. If, any second, God could start talking."

The man with the medals is shouting and every cry wraps

around the elephant's wing and the butterfly's hoof. The mutant of Calia's drawing could take any of the manifold forms God assumes when he refuses to speak and forsakes us.

The fly shits on another of the shouting man's medals. And another, and another.

The flies never stop shitting. For Calia, the flies are the butterflies that house's inhabitants deserve.

For my love story to be a true tragedy, worthy of a bard whose identity remains debated even among the foremost scholars of Elizabethan dramaturgy, for it to have the backstitching of a proper domestic drama, there had to be an escape, then pursuit by a domineering father. The father isn't evil in domestic dramas because, within that genre, in the interest of greater realism, all characters are shades of gray, bright fabrics nuanced by dark threads, or vice versa. It's disappointing. And annoying, because Dad doesn't even have the balls to let me be a tragic heroine. You can see on his face that he has no clue what kind of discipline to impose or how his kids have been raised. He's just figuring it out now and internally regretting it because he has always put his uniform before domestic responsibilities. For me, this inspires both pity and rage. Pity, because he really does want to be a good father, he just doesn't know how, he can barely bring himself to hold my thong between his index finger and thumb; he tries to put it between my hands, to return the object sticky with sweat and God-knows-what intimate secretions. It's an appalling realization; he's disgusted by the thong and disgusted by this encounter with his daughter's genital privacy. I should be compassionate and deal with it. I should but I don't. There's rage where my compassion ought to be, okay? So what if I'm trying to be the heroine of this story. That doesn't mean I have to be kind or gracious. Not necessarily. I could even be an antiheroine: dark fabric with bright back-stitching, a totally realistic character who doesn't hate her father but isn't eager to make things easy for him either.

As he attempts to return my thong, Dad sways back and forth, hunches over, looks old as fuck. Old and worn. I think it's from the weight of the medals, aging objects that clank and jangle in concert, turning him into a splinter of a man. Long-term exposure to heavy medals can accelerate age-related deterioration.

Uh-huh. You can see it in the stitching. All things considered, he's a pretty mediocre character. He always wanted to be a father so he could shatter the myth, shatter the idea that soldiers can't be gentle with their offspring, no matter how detestable or disgusting those offspring might be.

I'm both, for the record.

Dad finally decides to put the thong down on a chair, with a motion so careful it seems artificial, rehearsed, choreographed, excessive. I'd rather he just hit me instead of looking at me with those bugged-out fly eyes.

"Cacasandra . . ."

Caca-sandra. Every time. The ineluctable fecal prefix.

"Cacasandra, you were the pick of the litter . . ."

There's so much disappointment in his voice that I feel bad for him.

Almost, anyway.

Pick of the litter. Those were the words he chose. There were any number of ways to phrase that sentiment. For example, he could have said you were the best of my children, you were my favorite, you were the apple of my eye, and still he chose *those* words, made me the most beloved bitch in a group of runty puppies, and to top it off, he adds the fecal prefix, as usual.

Just call me a good girl and toss me a bone, okay?

I'm not trying to be a linguistic purist or anything, but look, if we're trying to make this a tragedy or a domestic drama, Dad has chosen to communicate his ideas in the worst possible way. And now to the tally of his misdeeds, we must add the lifting of his index finger, the classic authoritarian gesture he made so famous at parades and in photo ops with Pop-Pop Mustache.

"Cacasandra, it's dididisgusting! It's shameful!"

"I love her."

Uh-huh. You can see in his scrunched-up face that he's having digestive issues. I have no choice but to assume my role as tragic heroine with whatever dignity I've been allowed to retain. A declaration of love doesn't solve anything—at least not anything for Dad, who's still squirming through a series of grimaces—but at least it'll act as a solid dramatic platform on which the conflict can unfold. Pulling this shit off isn't easy, okay? I'm not exactly dealing with Elizabethan characters conceived by a literary genius; I'm stuck with a herd of low-functioning family members getting shepherded around by the sound of Dad's voice.

"How long have you knoknown about this?" he asks with a cry, and I still haven't fully figured out which is worse, his volume or his inquisitorial tone.

He doesn't wait for me to reply, and I realize the question was a shot in the air, intended for this domestic drama's passive observers, namely Mom and Caleb, who are watching the scene without moving so much as a finger, but whose self-satisfied expressions suggest none of this is news to them. For example, Mom is wearing her best smile, the smile of an orgasmless woman who has a dish of nice cold revenge she's ready to eat in small, deliberate bites. Even Calia lifts her head for a second, emerges from her art and narrows her gaze on a specific object: my thong, fuchsia and resplendent like an object from another dimension atop the somber living room's gray furniture.

"She has been demonstrating certain deviations in her sexual conduct for . . . ," Mom replies, straining to remember, ". . . some time now."

"How long?"

"A while," she finally says with the voice of a consumptive sparrow, a voice that feigns maternal concern but isn't fooling anyone, a voice that doesn't possess the faintest trace of subtlety, and which amuses me with its restrained theatricality.

My knees hurt a little, so I sit down on top of my fuchsia thong. Calia immediately loses all interest in it and, still in her elephant period, returns to her drawings. Meanwhile Dad paces like he's marching in a parade. Seeing him with no uniform, but with the medals pinned to his shirt anyway, feels anachronistic and a little ridiculous. There are protocols that lose all meaning outside of a specific time and place. A fat fly lands on his forehead. They're funny, the flies. They can smell conflict a mile away.

Mom offers a half-hearted excuse:

"You were never here. I thought the problem would've resolved itself by now."

Uh-huh. I'm the dilemma. Cacasandra is the dilemma. Mom plays her card masterfully, venomously: she knows when to talk and when to keep silent. And now she's silent, doesn't make a peep; the role of inquisitor has moved elsewhere, to the corner of the ring known as Dad.

"I love her," I proffer in a barely audible voice. Despite

everything, Dad hears my voice, which provokes an indignant grimace. "She's my girlfriend."

"A bridge is your girlfriend, Cacasandra?"

Dad's question flies through the air, and Caleb laughs.

Bad idea.

Dad's eyes strike him down.

"There is bad blood in this house. Bad blood!"

Then he rambles incoherently, marching across the living room. Double time. Medals tinkling.

His head jostles as if he were an enormous terry-cloth marionette, and suddenly, to Mom, he spews:

"You dididn't see her! She was there, outside, in front of everyone! She has bad blood! Rancid blood! Totouching herself on the bridge. Look, look at this!"

He scans for the fuchsia thong, which has temporarily disappeared under the weight of my butt cheeks. I shift in my seat so everyone can see. Dad and his scrupulous fingers seize the garment, which he waves back and forth like the flag of a nation of sexual deviants.

"On the bridge and with nonothing underneath!"

I think it's the first time in his life that Dad is talking about something that isn't strictly related to politics or his political ascent. And even though my genitals are, to me, the most political thing in the world, I don't aspire to anything so lofty, I don't aspire to Dad ever understanding, okay? I'm not that stupid.

"I love her," I proffer every time Dad's screams seem to be abating. Got to keep the flames burning bright.

"Listen to her! Listen to your daudaughter! She says she loves a bridge! She talks about the bridge like it's fefefemale!" he spews at my mother again.

If Calia could depict Dad's mind, it would be an abstract work. A line piercing a triangle over here, a splotch in the corner, lots of smudges. I don't know which displeases Dad more: that I'm pining for a bridge, or that the object of my desire has a feminine essence. He can't decide either, but he swings my fuchsia thong from side to side as a symbol of my depravation.

Finally, he comes up to me.

All right, now's when the play takes on tragic backstitching.

His face is centimeters from mine.

He says:

"Even if it means tearing your head off, I'm going to mamake you nonononormal, Cacasandra."

"I love her."

"Cacacalm down."

Caca-calm.

"You can keep me away from her," I whisper, "you can lock me up, you can tear off my head, you can do whatever you like to me, but it won't change anything. I love her."

I know it's cliché, okay? I'm not pretending my speech is some highly literary monologue, full of fancy metaphors. But it's enough to make Dad's head—the abstract painting—explode.

"This house is fufull of poopoor morality and dedeviant behavior! These are seserious problems! Bad blood!"

Mom shrugs. She gets the hint, knows he's criticizing her.

"A house is a small cocountry. And a family is a nananation. A nananananation!"

The same dull political speechifying as always. Mom yawns. Caleb daydreams. Calia continues being Calia.

"Discipline! What this cocountry needs is discipline. I'm

cracking the whip! I'm taking the reins! Together we will pupull the carriage of our family out of the gulch! I'm going to save you no matter what it takes, Cacasandra."

"I love her," I repeat, and even though they're the same words as before, Dad becomes exasperated.

"Discipline is the foundation of the nananation! It's the foundation of everything! And nono one is better equipped than me to guide you back to the path of dedemocracy and peapeapeace!"

Peepee-peace.

In one of the corners of the room, my brother coughs inoffensively. But the sound sets off the alarms within the abstract painting of Dad's thoughts.

"Honor, shame, and glory! We shall prevail!" he declares. "Down with bad blood! Honor, shame, and glory!" he repeats, adding, "I will guide this country to redemption!"

The speech leaves a bittersweet taste in my mouth. Dad waves around my thong, which, between his hands, looks more like a banner for lost causes than ever. His fingers have lost their scruples. They touch my sweat and sink into the traces of rust my beloved left on the surface of the fabric.

"This family needs a great leader. You don't know me, no, not yet. But you will, you will have time, all the time in the world," Dad threatens, and with those words, his speech concludes with nary a stutter.

They met at a parade. Mom was wearing high-top boots. They were not quite her size, which made her limp and gave her an air of lightness and guilelessness that all the other girls in more appropriately sized boots envied.

"Bliblisters?" asked the man, who back then was anything but Dad.

Mom, who at that time was just a prettyish young woman with a limp, nodded with a smile. She recognized his face immediately. How could she not? It struck her as odd that he was there, exposed, amidst a multitude of men and women in uniform, as if he were a foot soldier among his comrades, as if he had forgotten his rank. That day, for the first time in her life, Mom felt important. Before meeting Dad, she had merely existed, just another young woman in uniform in the swarm of the country's endless summer, with no outward trait that gave her away, no outward trait that suggested her origins. Mom had taken great pains to fit within the national homogeneity because she knew heterogeneity came at a great price. Ever since her family had settled on suicide, ever since the appearance of the butterflies, and ever since the voice of her aunt—which is to say, the voice of God using her aunt's vocal cords as his amphora—gave way to a poison-induced death rattle, orphan-Mom knew she bore a stigma: the taboo of ancestral bad blood.

She could not remember what happened after the mass

suicide. There were butterfly wings fluttering overhead, but from that moment on, it was all a blur, a smoke screen over her memories. It was better that way. Forgetting was preferable. In her moment of need, the nation did not abandon her. Orphan-Mom was taken to one of many homes for parentless, undesirable, or otherwise exiled children, which is to say, she was sent to a democratic home, a reflection of exactly what the country wanted for all its citizens. Orphan-Mom endeavored to forget her misfortune as quickly as possible. It was important for her to adapt to these new circumstances, and she succeeded, to the point that she forgot the biological stain she bore, the suicidal flock from which she had come, thanks to her continuous attempts to fit into the jigsaw puzzle of the world.

Many psychologists and psychiatrists took their time speaking to orphan-Mom. They convinced her that any trauma could be overcome with science. Those butterflies of death, the ones she thought she saw lifting straight off the paper through the work of some dark influence, had never been real. There is nothing in this world that logic cannot explain. There is nothing in this world that the word *trauma* cannot explain. The eyes see what they want to see, and to be sure, children's eyes are especially susceptible. That was why Mom forced herself to erase the memory of those butterflies. In her mind, they had never existed. The psychiatrists and psychologists smiled and patted her on the head. Good girl. Very good girl. Once again, the world of logic had emerged victorious over the chaos of obscurantism.

And from that point on, everything was nearly perfect.

Nearly, because every time orphan-Mom closed her eyes, those hateful butterflies reappeared. They were still there, under the filing cabinet, hiding between folders of psychological evaluations, camouflaged during hours of therapy. Persistent motherfuckers. But to forget, she merely had to open her eyes. The world immediately returned to its standard rotation on the same axis, day after day.

But the reality was very different, as she knew perfectly well: the butterflies were still there, in the deepest recesses of her memory.

Orphan-Mom did not like military boots, and she did not care for parades. It was exhausting, dragging your feet in boots that almost seemed designed for discomfort. Her blisters grew. Her feet began to lag behind. She did not do it on purpose. All orphan-Mom wanted was to be part of the swarm, to be a homogenous young woman, which, if you think about it, should not have been so difficult even for a girl like her, a girl without a family, raised in a democratic nest for outcasts. The nation had ensured circumstances were optimal; anyone who tried could be an equal, could be the same: the same clothes, the same uniforms, the same ideas, the same heat, the same summer that warmed the same parts of their bodies. Standard-issue citizens pulling themselves up by the straps of their standard-issue boots. Blisters were the only thing that made Mom different. Limping made her different. But that was her lucky day.

"Booboots too small?" asked the man, the soldier whose face she knew from memory. He did not strike her as especially attractive, but power takes unusual forms and can sometimes resemble beauty, and when orphan-Mom looked at the man, she found him charming. She had never imagined that a soldier of his rank could stutter that way, so tenderly, an important man revealing that he was nervous, human, imperfect. Mom's feet were not the only thing failing.

"The opposite," she replied. "They're a size too big."

"Then let's go get you some new boobooboots. You can't mamarch like that."

If orphan-Mom had been given a choice, she would not have put any boots on her feet, regardless of their size or condition. She would have worn high heels, red, the kind that cause real blisters. When Mom pictured herself atop shoes like stilts, in her mind, she was the most beautiful woman in the world. Of course, thoughts like these were off-limits back then, at least for her, for a girl striving to be homogenous and eschew difference. Back then, the prospect of new boots, of getting to know this stately stutterer, was beyond her wildest dreams.

She followed him through the crowd. Without saying a word.

The stately stutterer's bodyguard fixed his eyes on orphan-Mom.

"This guy fofollows me everywhere," Dad said. No further explanation necessary.

They got married two months later, and by then, orphan-Mom was pregnant with Cacasandra and had already renounced orgasms for life. Dad gave her a beautiful pair of heels. They were black, not red, and she felt that such a gift represented happiness in its purest form. She could not wear them though; her feet were too swollen from the pregnancy. Even in utero, Cacasandra was a bad daughter: she gave her mother morning sickness, twitches, bloating. Orphan-Mom tried to squeeze her feet into the high-heel shoes, and that was frustration in its purest form.

"They don't fit," she guiltily confessed to Dad.

"You and your feefeet," he replied, "always so cocompli-cated."

She never loved him. That stately stutterer was always busy with matters of political and national importance, always trying to climb one rung higher on the ladder of duty, always taking care of his medals. Mom focused on her children, her self-help books, and her shoe collection. For her, that was love: a pair of new heels, the promise that she would never have to wear boots or march with blistered feet again.

Caleb went downstairs and pulled the dead sparrow from his pocket. It was in pretty bad shape, basically pulp. Too bad. It would not fit in his puzzle. Frustrating. All that effort for nothing. All that effort just for pulp. Their bodies were not very durable and Caleb had been pressing his weight against the wall while Dad droned on, while Casandra repeated the same thing over and over, insisting on her love, stinking like a rusty nail, a smell that apparently no one in the family could detect except him.

The image of Casandra's fuchsia thong was etched in his mind. It was a memory that gave him a nervous, strange sensation. If his big sister wore underwear like that, maybe Tunisia did too. The name, the memory of his cousin gave Caleb goosebumps. It was not hard to imagine Tunisia wearing that fuchsia thong. Tunisia smelling like a rusty nail.

It was better not to think about her, the girl with the eyeglasses.

Tunisia was off-limits.

Caleb knew he would never see her again, now that her parents were enemies of the people.

That summer threatened to be long and stifling.

He forced himself to think about the sparrow, or rather, about the pulp with wings and something resembling a beak. He wanted to add it to his masterpiece.

That was when he heard someone clearing her throat, just above his shoulder. The smell of rust wafted up his nose.

"What are you doing down here?" he asked. "Aren't you grounded?"

"Uh-huh. So?"

His big sister grimaced in disgust when she noticed the dead sparrow. Caleb braced for some hateful comment, but Casandra bit her lip and said nothing.

It was Caleb, ultimately, who couldn't stand the silence any longer. "What do you want?"

"Dad has gone crazy. Haven't you noticed? Please say yes."

"You're the crazy one, bridgefucker."

"Uh-huh, whatever, Sparrowkiller Caleb." Casandra sighed. "I'm being serious. If you don't help me—"

"Stop. Leave me alone. I'm busy."

"Dad has lost his shit. If you don't see it, that's your problem. He wants to become Pop-Pop Mustache. Do you know what that means?"

". . . I don't care."

"He's gonna do experiments on us, Caleb. Basically the same as Pop-Pop Mustache. Except Pop-Pop was experimenting with a country."

"You're the one experimenting. You're in love with a fucking bridge. Leave me alone."

"Guys like Dad don't give up their power. You have to take it from them."

Caleb choked on a cackle.

"So, besides being a bridgefucker, you're an enemy of the people now too?"

Casandra shrugged.

"You don't know Pop-Pop Mustache, Caleb. Not like me. Imagine if Dad starts acting like that. Your whole life will be fucked. So will mine. Even Calia's. You don't get it. You have no idea what this means. There'll be new laws that—"

"Leave me alone."

"Why are you such an idiot? Guys like Dad are dangerous. He's lost everything. They took away everything. We're all he has left. Don't you get it?"

"I said I don't care. Leave me alone."

Casandra poked the dead sparrow.

"Okay, whatever, that's on you, but you're gonna regret it. Dad has gone crazy. And it's gonna be a long summer, Caleb. Don't say I didn't warn you."

Caleb did not stop to think about what Casandra said. Honestly, he was more concerned with remembering Tunisia, the bespectacled cousin lost to him forever. He was more concerned with imagining a fuchsia thong. And with trying to find somewhere to cram that sparrow into his puzzle of dead animals.

Why don't you like butterflies, Mom?"

"Because they're harbingers of death."

"How do you know . . . ?"

"My aunt told me."

"Are you scared of them?"

"Of butterflies? A little. That's why I don't mind that you kill them."

"I don't! They—"

"I know, Caleb, you already told me . . . they seek you out, they touch you, and that's all. They fall. They commit suicide. I know, I know."

"But it's true."

"So, is what your sister told me also true?"

"The bunny died."

"Caleb, you can be honest with Mommy. Do you like torturing defenseless little animals?"

"No!"

"If you keep information from Mommy, she can't help you."

"I don't do anything to them."

"Do you poison them? Kick them?"

"No!"

"Does it feel good when you do that?"

"They die, that's all. It's not my fault."

"Of course not. No one said it was your fault. Me, I don't

like butterflies. I consider them odious insects and I'd rather they didn't exist."

"But they're pretty."

"Tell me what happened that day at the zoo."

"I went with Dad and Casandra. The animals were weird. Dad yelled."

"Did you feel scared?"

"No, just like, a jolt."

"A jolt?"

"Yeah, I always feel a shock when they touch me and die. Why do they want to die?"

"Caleb, the first thing you have to understand is that animals don't think."

"Yes, they do. They think about dying."

"How do you know?"

"I can tell."

"Do the animals talk to you?"

"No."

"So how can you be so sure?"

"Because when they touch me and fall down, they feel better."

"The animals . . . ?"

"Yeah."

"They feel better about what?"

"About not being alive. They like that."

"The question is if you like them not being alive."

"They're pretty when they're dead."

"Say more."

"They stop moving. So you can see them better. When they're moving, it's hard to see the patterns on their fur, the colors . . . right? But when they're not moving, you can look at them as much as you want and they're prettier."

"You think death is pretty?"

"Yeah. When there are a lot of animals that have stopped moving, you figure something out . . ."

"And what's that?"

"They fit in each other."

"What do you mean?"

"Like, an ant can be on top of a baby bird, and the baby bird can be stuck into a rabbit. They're pretty on their own, but they're way more beautiful when they're together."

"Like a sculpture?"

". . . except sometimes they don't fit together good. It's hard. It's like a puzzle."

"So you kill them to build a—"

"They die on their own, I don't do anything."

"Can you show it to me?"

"Show you what?"

"Your puzzle."

"How do you know if I—"

"You just told me. And anyway, I'm your mother. I'm supposed to know everything that's happening."

"All right. Follow me."

"Where?"

"Downstairs."

"The puzzle is hidden?"

"Yeah."

"Hm. Are there butterflies?"

"A few . . . are you scared?"

"It's fine."

"They're dead though, Mom. If they're dead, they can't hurt you. They're just pretty, that's it."

"All right."

"Mom . . . ?"

"Yes?"

"It really isn't my fault. Are you mad at me?"

"No."

"Are you mad at the butterflies?"

"Sometimes, but not right now. Is your sister's bunny part of your puzzle? Tell me the truth, Caleb."

"Just the ears."

"Just the ears?"

"They were the only part that fit."

Many complained of the country's blistering heat, of the endless, boundless summers. Dad knew that these shapeless, seemingly inoffensive comments camouflaged the antipatriotic notions of the enemies of the people, the enemies of democracy, the enemies of General Mustache. A criticism of the country's climate was a criticism of the country and its government. Dad was a simple man. He accepted summer as another of the many things that required no explanation and against which it was better not to fight. He endured the flies, the sweat running in rivulets between his skin and his shirt, even the rust on his medals. He did not understand Mom, who was always fanning herself with a palm frond or the nearest newspaper, who was always lifting her blouse to get more air. The summer could be stifling, sure, but it had its upsides. You need look no farther than the beach; not least of the country's many advantages were its beaches, the most beautiful in the world, where the sea meets the shore and children can frolic, happy and healthy, places that Casandra had adored since she was two years old.

A lot of time had passed between toddler Casandra playing in the sand and teenage Casandra humping the bridge. Dad was coming to understand what old folks had always said: time waits for no man. There he was, in his country, watching time lay waste to everything it touched: his family, his dreams, his rungs of power. However corrosive they might be, the years cannot be faulted; that has always been their purpose, since the dawn of time, which is to say, for far longer than Dad has been paying attention to such matters.

Melancholy.

A soldier cannot be a melancholy creature, Dad reprimanded himself. Or rather, the military voice in his head reprimanded him. But it barely makes a difference anymore, the same voice thought in a slightly less domineering tone. A soldier can let himself be vulnerable when no one is looking, and this was just such a moment, a moment of liberation, when Dad could allow himself a nostalgic tear or two over the daughter he had lost, over that daughter's transformation into yet another thing he did not understand. Or perhaps—who says he's not allowed?—Dad can even cry about the tragedies of the past year, about the precipitous fall from grace so destructive that the world had come crashing down around him.

When a certain Adam and Eve—or whoever you like, dealer's choice—were expelled from the Garden of Eden, aka the Garden of Power, they had to start from square one, learn how to exist in this new reality where God was absent except as a distant presence. Though he would never equate himself to the original sinners—Dad had never committed the sin of treason—he shared in what they must have felt: wandering a no-man's-land with no guide or goal, with no hope of ascending one rung higher on the ladder of glory.

Dad had been orphaned of a nation, orphaned of ideas.

And now, too, orphaned of his children.

It is true he had not been a perfect father, your classic Good Dad who never misses a birthday or a graduation. He was a distant presence. His medals opened many doors, doors through which his children and wife were constantly walking; for all their talk, they cashed in on the perks of power without remorse. Notwithstanding his absence, Dad had tried to be good, to love his loved ones. There was not a soul alive who could say he had done otherwise.

Caleb had never been close to Dad; he was an aloof child adrift in the currents of his own thoughts who preferred to ride the waves of his mind unaccompanied. He was also kind of a freak. Dad could never forget that afternoon years earlier, those death-bent zoo animals. And Calia, well, better not to talk about her. Granted, small children are rarely interesting. They never talk about anything exciting. They are focused on their biological processes: eating, crapping, sleeping, eating, crapping, screaming; but without hesitation, Dad would have preferred an unexceptional, boring daughter, a run-of-the-mill sleeper and eater and crapper, to his miniature savant spawn, this silent genie of the lamp. Chills. Dad got chills whenever that child was close.

Casandra was different.

Dad felt genuine love for her. Or, at least, he performed an authentic form of love. He knew no other way, and we must give credit where credit is due; he loved Casandra because, of all his children, only she seemed normal. Add to this that Casandra had been, for years, the apple of General Mustache's eye, a sort of granddaughter to whom the General paid tribute, which in some sense linked Dad not only to power, but to its source.

If only Casandra had remained that girl forever.

But alas.

Dad felt the sweat running down his neck.

He had lost the prospect not only of power but of any sort of future. And he knew it. You do not climb your way up from the bottom of the well. He had given up all hope from the first moment. Dad would not live his life clinging to the salty crumbs of hope.

He was a man with his feet planted firmly on the ground.

So many years in military service teach a man, forcibly, the need to be practical.

A stab of resentment in his chest.

Fucking heat. Fucking Casandra.

"I am the master of this house," he said, building himself up. "And I reek of rancid blood! I will show them how to govern this nation!"

He was beginning to understand . . . the signs had been there all along, but he hadn't been a practical man back then, much less a lover of beauty. Who says a soldier can't be a lover of beauty? That girl at the parade, with her oversize boots and blisters on her feet, the woman who fantasized about high-heel shoes, had brought misfortune upon him. Dad did not have to justify his decisions in the name of love. He had never loved her. He had merely thought he saw something beautiful in her body, thought she would give him beautiful children, children who would conquer the world. On the scale of life, beauty was the perfect counterbalance to power.

Even practical men make mistakes, including the fatal kind.

And it was too late to rectify. The children were beautiful, yes, he could credit their mother with that. They had inherited her predisposition for beauty along with everything else, and everything else was quite a lot, an ocean of secrets and defects.

How had he missed it? His wife was pretty, but she had suicide in her blood, and Dad knew there was no fixing a person's DNA.

Fucking DNA. Fucking summer. Fucking country.

No, fucking country, no. The country didn't do anything wrong.

It was his fault. He had been the author of his own downfall and now he was paying for it in flesh and bones, flesh of his flesh and bone of his bones, his three defects: the Crayola savant, the bunnykiller, and the girl with the fuchsia thong.

But Dad was a practical man. He knew perfectly well that you reach the final rung of power not with self-pity but with an iron fist, a hand capable of meting out punishment and reward. He had been watching, and he had been learning. General Mustache was a great teacher, the greatest of them all.

Fucking sweat.

He was no longer General Mustache's favorite. Or anyone else's. Many times, he had been tapped to be the General's successor when biology and the passage of time handed down their final verdict. Everyone knew General Mustache was not immortal. But fate is a bitch. Fate is a filthy, backstabbing bitch who had betrayed Dad, the man who had loved her most. Now General Mustache was left with no successor and Dad was left with no future, no hope, no legacy.

The only nation he truly had left was his home, his family of defectives. And Dad had every intention of establishing irrevocable order and perfection throughout the land.

At first the changes were imperceptible. It was almost impossible to imagine what Dad had in mind. Credit where credit is due; I knew it from the beginning, and if you don't believe me, you can ask Caleb, if he remembers and has the balls to tell you. I didn't venture down to his little dead-bunny nest and put on a loving-older-sister routine for shits and giggles. Extending an olive branch isn't easy, okay? Just the thought of being near my disgusting little brother gave me goosebumps, and that ought to show you just how desperate the circumstances had become. Alliances are complicated, that's true in every story and this one's no exception. First off, there had yet to be a true conflict, genuine friction between two parties, and my premonition, though accurate, wasn't good enough.

Caleb would have time to regret it, and I would have time to play the true role I was born to play: tragic heroine.

Uh-huh. It was tragedy enough being torn from the object of my affection, but as the bards like to say, there's nothing better than a thwarted passion, because then the passion runneth over and maketh a big mess. Feeling my beloved's rust against my skin, the touch of her beam against my body, wasn't enough for me. My father, as the chief obstacle to our love's consummation, had become a dirty old man, my story's public enemy number one. He locked me in my bedroom, screamed blah dee blah and fa-la-la, and refused to give back my fuchsia thong.

"You're to stay in here until further notice," he said, slamming the door.

Even then, I didn't notice he had stopped stuttering. It's the rage, it makes me blind to that kind of thing. I'm not perfect, okay? The disappearance of the stutter was the first indication of the microscopic transformation underway within my father's body, a metamorphosis that progressed little by little, step-by-step, all summer long.

But at that point we still had no idea. I had no idea.

Summer had just begun. I thought his tantrum would run its course after a few days and then he'd open the door again and blah dee blah dee blah. A man like Dad never allows violence to get the better of him. Oh, little naïve me. This story's tragic heroine is a little slow on the uptake. Dad decided that his dictatorship would begin then and there.

Summer had made the same decision.

Summer's dictatorship brought more flies and sweat, but at least that was predictable.

Dad's screams alternated with Casandra's fits of rage. One door would open, another would slam. The hinges creaked with fury. Being an insect was preferable to living in that house. But venturing outside was impossible and not only because of the heat, which one could mitigate by standing under a shady tree or simply endure—there were other reasons. The outside world no longer existed, at least not for the moment; it was another dimension, an inaccessible parallel universe.

Which was, to say the least, unfair. Caleb needed to find new animals so he could finish his masterpiece. Now, with the hellish heat, his installation of corpses was decomposing more rapidly, and from time to time, the putrefaction would waft up to the living room, prompting Dad to exclaim:

"It reeks in here! It's smelled like shit in this house all summer," and then he would scan the outside world through one of the windows, carefully, stealthily, so no one would see him—a watchful or a nosy eye, an emissary of General Mustache, or merely a neighbor taking cruel delight in Dad's tragedy as it unfolded.

Since Caleb could no longer go to the garden, his artwork remained unfinished. Which was a travesty, considering the puzzle was nearly complete. But the situation was out of his control. Dad did not waste his time on Caleb. To him, the boy was just another teenager, albeit one to whom he was bound by certain genetic characteristics: a few common features, such as the hawk nose, black hair, and excessively white skin nevertheless devoid of freckles, skin not suitable for anyone living in a land with so much sun, a country with so much summer that skin ages fast. Dad himself appeared older than he was, with nearly white hair and wrinkles around his lips and on his forehead.

"It reeks in here! It's smelled like shit in this house all summer."

More than a few times, Caleb caught Dad leaning out the window. Usually the windows were all locked, and he kept the keys someplace secret. "I will unlock the house when this family learns the meaning of the words *order* and *civilization*."

From time to time, Dad would say, "I smell rot," then scrutinize the dark night through the window. He was certain that the smell had been planted by the neighbors, who had no doubt placed bags full of shit in the garden, motivated by malice to commit an antipatriotic hate crime. He never said this, but Caleb and the others knew that is what he thought.

People have bad blood in times of disgrace. They relish and laugh at their neighbors' downfalls, their neighbors' tragedies. *They used to fear me*, Dad thought, *and now they bury sacks of shit on my property*.

Soon, Caleb noticed Dad had stopped stuttering. He did not mention this discovery to anyone, but it struck him as a bizarre, disquieting change. He had gotten used to his father's drawn-out syllables, to being called Cacaleb instead of Caleb, and truth be told, he didn't mind the *caca*. It was worse, he thought, that Dad had stopped stuttering, that he now called him Caleb, just like that—clean, omitting the fecal prefix with which Caleb had come to identify.

Despite all this, the boy was not miserable. The heat was the same as always, or maybe a little worse because the house was sealed off, the doors all locked and the windows sealed shut, a blockade only Dad's eyes dared violate. He wished he could finish his puzzle, but he did not feel especially worried, because Dad had already found a culprit for the smell pervading the house. The neighbors' shitbags had created a garden of metaphorical waste in Dad's mind, and now they fertilized the terrain of his ideas and suspicions.

More annoying was Casandra. Only those who have an older sister will truly understand Caleb's sentiments. She had shut herself away in her bedroom and only occasionally came downstairs clad in nothing but her underwear, a peculiar parade of red, purple, and green thongs. Caleb would look at Casandra's skinny legs with scorn and then immediately wonder if Tunisia's legs were skinny like that, like little flamingo legs. That was when Casandra's red thong became Tunisia's red thong—did she wear thongs like that? Skimpier ones? Were hers colorful too, or were they black and white?

Dad's screams alternated with Casandra's, and Caleb stopped thinking about Tunisia. How could he think about Tunisia when there was so much noise?

"Let me out! I have to see my love!" Casandra cried melodramatically.

"Over my dead body, young lady."

"Open the door. I hate you. You're a pig!"

"Perversions of a sexual nature—of any nature!—will be severely punished in this home. We will not brook dissidence of any kind."

"You're not in charge of me, okay? You're not my father, you're a fucking nobody. And you're not General Mustache!"

"Bad blood!" Dad howled and, immediately, he sought the evasive eyes of his wife, who was strutting around in red stilettos and opening, with forced casualness, a new book on psychoanalysis or a biography of Freud.

Mom was not concerned with Casandra. Nor was she concerned with Dad's howling or Caleb's stinking puzzle in the basement. In fact, at that exact moment, Mom was focused solely on watching Calia. Her youngest would soon turn three, in that midsummer madness, locked in that house. The fact that her daughter's third birthday would take place during the familial incarceration, following Dad's fall from the zenith of power to the swamps of indigence, was not keeping her up at night.

Something else was.

Coincidence or not, Caleb also noticed the change in Calia's drawings.

"I think the elephant period just ended," he announced on a day like any other, with a shrug, as if he were conveying harmless information without life-and-death implications. "I wonder what'll come next."

On Calia's white sheets of paper, they began to see the early studies, the early sketches of long, slender insect bodies. They were not yet anatomically precise, but they had wings, and the wings had colors. Mom stifled a scream as she looked at the sheets on which Calia had begun to draw.

"It's her butterfly period," she whispered. There was panic in her voice.

Caleb shrugged again.

"Huh. Does that mean we're all gonna die?"

The myths and legends we are told in childhood are always ghastly. Grown-ups go to great lengths to give their moral fables a sharp backstitching of terror. These are the stories that are etched in the genome of our minds and keep us up at night. It is ironic that parents wonder why their kids cry, why their kids cannot sleep. Because parents are idiots; it is clear as can be, only a fool would fail to see the boogeyman under the box spring, the devil in the dancing shoes, the butterflies that burst to life and break free from their white-paper prison.

Butterflies were the messengers of death who visited the drawings of misfits and child geniuses and, occasionally, took on the voice of God, the voice of a relative. Butterflies were terrible insects better kept at an arm's length, trapped in all their anatomical perfection within Calia's drawings.

Mom cannot be faulted for talking about her childhood trauma. Her progeny was not her preferred audience for such stories, but she simply had no one else to talk to, and the kids, as fate or genetic fluke would have it, lived under her roof. In other words, it is impossible for children to escape their parents and their parents' terrors. The tale of the butterflies had been a part of them for as long as they could remember.

By this point in life, the kids knew Mom did not love them.

The beauty of it was that the kids did not love her either.

It was the reciprocal absence of a feeling that, though it seemed fundamental in books about happy families, had little bearing in the real world. Tolerance, on the other hand, was of the utmost importance to maintaining equilibrium within the home. Mom managed, barely, to endure the children and their more freakish qualities, and the children endured the woman in the heels, the genetic incubator who continually attempted to fix them through a battery of self-help books and senseless questioning.

It was a delicate balance and, at times, an almost happy one.

There was a silent pact between them, formed without the mediation of words, forged only through a common fear that haunted their dreams. For as long as Calia had shown a precocious knack for art, the entire family had been keeping an eye on their child genius. And on her creations. They analyzed hairs on elephant trunks and the many butts of monkey mating season. When Calia moved on to the fractal designs of insect still lifes, they searched for wings, the sign that she had become a vessel of death or a messenger of God.

In other words, everyone was spying on Calia.

Which is not so strange; in this country, spying on your neighbor, your daughter, or your baby sister is a matter of trifling importance, the most boring and commonplace of domestic tasks. And the family did it well.

Very well, in fact . . . until that day.

"Does that mean we're all gonna die?" Caleb asked when he saw the first wings appear on Calia's pages.

"Of course not," Mom replied, but her eyes gave her away.

It was Mom who gathered up all of Calia's paper and crumpled them into balls, shapeless piles, then she exploded:

"Leave me in peace! Leave me alone! What else do you want from me?" She grabbed Calia by the chin and forced her daughter to look into her eyes.

Calia protested with a grimace and an indistinct sound and attempted to wrest control of the paper balls Mom had snatched from her.

"I'm going to burn your fucking butterflies, you hear me, you little freak? I'm going to burn them to fucking ashes."

Credit where credit is due: Calia did not look at her mother with malice, as a possessed child in a horror movie would, nor did she howl in the darkness, transform into a werewolf, or express her rage in any way. She merely clutched the pencils in her two fists, in case Mom tried to take those away too.

Dad had always hated mustaches. They struck him as untidy. A lush, beautiful mustache required a lot of free time. Otherwise, it was just formless fringe, too similar to a genital bush flourishing on the facial equator. Dad had no such time, and he shaved every day, a task that did not do his sensitive, wrinkled skin any favors, but which he accepted as a domestic ritual like any other.

But things had changed considerably. Now Dad had free time to make plans, even to monitor the nearly imperceptible progress of each hair sprouting slowly from his face.

He had been a fool for refusing to grow a mustache. It was, in fact, far more practical. Time to bid razor burn, rusty blades, and early-morning nicks and cuts farewell.

It was the first change of many: as the whiskers grew, Dad felt as if a bit of his lost power were returning to him, as if those small, still-shapeless hairs offered some form of consolation. He considered himself a man of action, a man of accelerated thought. He understood perfectly why the General had a mustache. It was not a question of aesthetic preference, it was a stroke of genius.

The mustache makes the man.

The mustache makes the man trustworthy.

The mustache, most of all, makes the man powerful.

It would be redundant to add: the mustache makes the man

capable of taking control, enforcing stability within a family or a nation.

Dad did not want to be just a man, he wanted to be a just man. He wanted his children to love him.

Powerful men know the practice of love always goes hand in hand with fear. We love what we fear, and vice versa.

The shadow of the mustache made him look younger, concealed his lips. Dad understood that the General was intelligent, wise, ahead of his time. Anyone who can move his mouth without exposing himself to lip-reading is always the victor and never the vanquished.

In the family, as in politics, it was important to make that distinction clear.

Dad was happy—for the first time in a long time, for the first time since his fall from grace—when that morning he gazed into the mirror and barely recognized himself. It was not his own face gazing back at him in the silver.

It was General Mustache's.

Guess what I have for you in this box."

"I dunno."

"Think about it, Casandrita. It's a gift for a beautiful young woman like you."

"A dress?"

". . . a flower-print dress. Do you like flowers?"

"They're okay."

"There's nothing more beautiful than a young woman in a floral dress, Casandrita. Do you want it?"

"Uh-huh, I guess."

"Open it. It's time to forget about those boring old dolls. They were pretty boring, right? Do you like the dress?"

"Uh-huh."

"Hm. So you don't like it. That's all right, you don't have to lie. Sometimes it seems like you're the only person in the world who's honest with old Pop-Pop Mustache. I don't expect much from the others, but from you—"

"I want something else."

"See? Now we're understanding each other."

"Your office chair."

"My chair? What's so special about my chair?"

"Everything."

"You like office chairs? Really? That much?"

"I'd die for that chair."

"Why?"

"Because I love it."

"Ah, yes, I understand. It's a very comfortable chair. I had a rifle once, and it was special too. I couldn't bear to be without it. It understood me. It was a natural extension of my arm. It was a marvelous, meticulous tool for blowing people's brains out . . . see, Casandrita? We just had our first conversation as two grown-ups."

"What does 'meticulous' mean?"

"It's a matter of squeamishness. I hate bloodstains, splattered guts. Killing isn't always comfortable."

"Did you love it?"

"Killing? Or are we talking about my rifle again?"

"Your rifle."

"For some strange reason, when you aimed for someone's head and squeezed the trigger, it did its work so cleanly it was practically surgical."

"Were you in love with it?"

"It was useful. You already have love on the mind, Casandrita?"

"Are you gonna give me your chair?"

"Well now, you are a quick one. Not so fast. Everything in life has its price, don't you think?"

"I guess."

"You're a keen observer, Casandra. You think I haven't noticed? You see everything. Curiosity is a wonderful trait. Some consider it a flaw, but your old Pop-Pop Mustache doesn't. Your old Pop-Pop Mustache is curious too. And do you know who I'm very, very curious about? Your father."

"Okay . . ."

"Everyone says he'll make an excellent successor. An excellent successor to *me* . . . what do you think, Casandrita? Have you heard anything about that?"

"No."

"How odd. Your father loves hearing opinions . . . you haven't even heard what your aunt and uncle think about that idea?"

"No. Are you gonna give me your chair?"

"Ah, no, we aren't talking about that right now. That chair . . . is very comfy. It's a natural extension of my ass. You don't want your Pop-Pop Mustache, at his advanced age, to make such a big sacrifice just to satisfy a childish whim, do you? Unless . . ."

"Unless what . . . ?"

"If you want that chair so much, you could listen a little more, pay closer attention to things. I'm not talking about obvious things, Casandrita, but tiny details. Details that are often overlooked. Do you understand?"

"I guess."

"'I guess' is a very ambiguous response. Let's be clear. I want you to listen meticulously every time your father talks to your aunt and uncle. You know how curious your Pop-Pop can be."

"You want me to be your spy?"

"No, Casandrita, absolutely not. What an ugly word! Such a harsh word coming from the clean mouth of a girl like you. I'm not asking that much. I'm proposing a fair trade, an exchange of two things of equal value. If you really want my wonderful office chair—"

"I'm in love with your office chair."

"Love is fleeting, but your Pop-Pop Mustache's affection is forever."

"Did Dad do something bad?"

"No, of course not. Who said that? Why so tense, Casandrita? Do you think that if your father were an enemy of the state, an enemy of the people, an enemy of Pop-Pop Mustache, he would still be alive? I don't doubt his loyalty. But I'm curious. And please, don't ever use that ugly word, spy, again. It hurts your old Pop-Pop's heart. A spy is an enemy of this country's achievements. There's a difference between a spy and an observer, can't you tell? An observer is a friend. A hero. Or in this case, a heroine."

He had no choice but to wait until nighttime. The doors were still locked and Dad had the key. At least when it was dark, his father showed fewer signs of vigilance. He did not sniff the air in search of nonexistent sacks of shit or quietly ruminate about revenge. If Dad were the sort of man who snored, Caleb could have acted with greater confidence, could have been more daring, might have even snuck into his bedroom and stolen the keys or taken some other last-minute action for a few instants of freedom. Caleb was not a rebel. In fact, he was not even sure he knew the meaning of the word, which, in that house, needless to say, was used rarely and always with a look of suspicion, lest rebelliousness calcify in the bones of the next generation.

For Caleb, escaping meant being able to go outside, to the formerly unremarkable, now off-limits garden, a radioactive area that, according to Dad's latest set of orders, was to be avoided at all costs. But whatever it took, Caleb needed to find a final piece for his puzzle, for the work of installation art he had been building ever since he discovered the suicidal tendencies he inspired in nearby animals. Art had given death a purpose, and that purpose was a gift.

A gift for Tunisia.

Caleb's puzzle had become a sort of phantasmagorical tribute to the cousin he had lost forever. He had never considered himself the type to make grand romantic gestures, but that is how life works—simmer confinement and hormones long enough, and you get a terrible concoction, perform acts of desperation. In any case, Caleb knew perfectly well that his gift would never reach its intended recipient.

The boy sighed.

He still thought about his cousin. So much that, sometimes, her characteristics blurred or melted into others within his imagination. Tunisia, too, had become a sort of mix-and-match puzzle, a pastiche of thick eyeglasses, Casandra's legs and underwear, and the odd element drawn from adolescent fantasy.

Caleb was not the kind of kid who had his feet or head in the clouds; in fact, he was quite practical. It did not take extraordinary intelligence to conclude that seeing Tunisia again was highly improbable, that she would end up dissolving into the abyss of disremembrance, that every day she would melt a little more into the images of Casandra and other girls Caleb remembered. Tunisia had been taken far away, to some remote corner of the country, branded the daughter of an enemy of the people—worse still, the daughter of two enemies of the people, two terrorists, two bombmakers.

Caleb's primary concern was not Calia and her butterflies, or the fear that pervaded the house, or his older sister's screams, or her parade of polychrome thongs. Caleb was concerned, more than anything else, about Dad and his metamorphosis.

This was something he did not want to think about. It was better not to let the idea take shape; he would rather wait it out. It was just two months until the end of summer, or rather, two months until the end of the period formally designated by the calendar as such within that geographic region. After that, Dad would have to let them out, he would have to let them go, because life goes on even after the fall. Even the children of powerless, disgraced, dethroned men had to be molded within the educational system of that perfect society in which all citizens are created equal, or at least created very similar.

He just needed to stay strong and practice patience, Caleb told himself with a shrug. As he did every night, he carefully studied the sounds of the house, the noises in the darkness, heightened by imagination.

Then, slowly, he opened his bedroom door.

He knew it was risky. Dad had enacted new laws. He had imposed a seven o'clock curfew because nighttime, he said, was for meditating on the day's misdeeds, which, as they all knew, were numerous, if not innumerable, in their family, rife as it was with sexual dissidents, loveless mothers, shoulder-shrugging teenagers, child geniuses.

Caleb did not consider himself a rebel. In fact, he thought obedience was preferable to defiance, thought a father satisfied with his own code of law was preferable to one seated in the corner, raging with single-minded fixation on his own downfall. If it were not for his unfinished puzzle, Caleb would have stayed put, would have patiently complied with the latest orders; summer does not last forever, even though sometimes it feels that way. But the puzzle beckoned, and Caleb had to turn that page, finish his monument to animal suicide, if only so he could stop thinking about Tunisia, his long-lost cousin whose memory grew more diffuse with each passing day.

He took the stairs one at a time. The creaking wood steps put his whole plan in jeopardy, and he had to move slowly. Downstairs, Caleb did not even try to open the door. He knew it would be pointless, and being the practical young man he was, he opted for the simplest solution: pressing against the wooden door as hard as possible, praying the nocturnal animals would smell or sense his presence and attempt to reach him.

His method yielded immediate results. The ants were the first to arrive. Big ones. Fat ones. Tiny ones. Winged ones. Black and red and brown ones. Caleb tried to shoo them away, his puzzle did not need more ants. It needed a larger body, something solid, a corpse he could tether to another corpse. The persistent ants tried to reach Caleb; the successful ones expired immediately. Others, he squashed.

With the ants came other insects. Finally, Caleb started to feel the cold, slimy skin of toads attempting to squeeze through the slit under the door. Toads were not ideal, but at least their bodies had some shape to them. He just needed to make contact.

There was a woof on the other side and Caleb's heart swelled.

"Good boy . . . shh, don't make noise. Come here, boy, shh."

There was no way the dog could squeeze through the slit under the door. That was clearly impossible, but in the heat of the moment, Caleb stopped thinking like the practical young man he was and allowed his feelings to get the best of him; he was blinded by his desire to forget about Tunisia and, more than that, his desire to finish the puzzle.

He stretched his fingers as far as he could. All the dog had to do was touch him, sniff him, lick those fingers, and it would be done, death would be served, his masterpiece would be complete.

That was a sloppy mistake. A mistake that, at any other moment, Caleb could have avoided.

"Come on, boy," he coaxed.

It was only when he looked up that he noticed Dad's presence. His lips were a mustache jungle. His father cleared his throat and lifted a boot. Then forcefully brought it down.

Caleb cried out.

It hurt.

Really fucking bad.

Dad pressed his boot down on Caleb's hand, pressed harder, and harder still, until the dog outside the house began to whimper and Caleb howled over and over.

"Rebel," Dad hissed. "Dissident." The syllables slipped out from under his mustache. "Now you're gonna sing for me nice and sweet, and believe me, you won't stop until I see blood."

In Caleb's hand, bones crunched.

'm glad you're back, Caleb. I've missed our little chitchats. What would you like to talk about today?"

"Nothing."

"You know that isn't true. You're here for a reason. You're a very practical young man."

"I want to tell you something. I want to tell you how much I hate you. How much we hate you."

"Whom else are you including when you say 'we'?"

"That's seriously your question?"

"What would you prefer, Caleb? I'd like to know. It will enable us to move forward with your therapy."

"It's not normal for a kid to hate his mother, is it?"

"It's more normal than you might think. All the books and scientific literature say so. In fact, the emotions typical of adolescence—"

"I hate you because you hate me."

"That's a broad generalization, Caleb, and rather abstract. You're lashing out with harsh language that reflects the state of your emotions, and that is leading you to absurd extremes. Have you heard of the law of the mirrors? It means you project what you are or what you feel onto someone else. Do you hate yourself, Caleb? Because what you see in me is nothing more than a reflection of your own thoughts, fears, and insecurities."

"Then tell me you love me. Say, 'I love you, Caleb, you're the most important thing in the world to me.'"

"Would it help you if I made that sort of statement?"

"If you meant it, yeah."

"Are you of the opinion that children must be the most important aspect of a woman's life?"

"Then why'd you have us?"

"You're working with an obsolete framework, Caleb. The fact of the matter is that babies are cute. They have big eyes and they look at the world with wonder. They have been expressly designed by nature to be adorable. That was my reason for having children. Then, babies grow. And just like that, the magic vanishes into nothing . . . and your father wanted children too. He made that clear on the day we met. He didn't use the word 'children,' he said 'descendants,' but that's more or less the same thing."

"It would be better if you said, 'I hate you, Caleb.'"

"Would you feel better if I made that sort of statement? Would it help you?"

"He crushed my hand."

"Your father has his quirks, Caleb. We all do. You, for example—"

"We're not talking about me. We're talking about him and you. He crushed my hand."

"You don't have a single broken bone."

"It hurt."

"Of course it hurt, Caleb. Military boots traditionally have hard soles. Did you really forget your father is a soldier?"

"Is that what he used to do outside? I mean before . . . before he was so important to Mustache."

"What do you mean?"

"Did he hit people? Break hands? Crush them? Is that what Dad did?"

"Your father's work was very serious, Caleb. He didn't have time for that sort of thing. Honestly, your imagination—"

"Did he hang people? Shoot them? Burn them? Did he like doing it like he liked crushing my hand?"

"Where are you getting these ideas?"

"How'd Dad get to be so important? Tell me!"

"Do you think terrorists and enemies of the people deserve your sympathy?"

"Why won't you answer me?"

"Because all you ask are stupid questions. What's the point of talking about these things, Caleb? It was a long time ago."

"What if he had trained dogs, Mom? Dogs that raped girls."

"That's horrible! Who told you that?"

"Did he really cut off guys' balls? Did he really make them eat their own balls?"

"No, of course that isn't true!"

"Did he really rip out people's teeth and nails? Did he really work in that place?"

"Caleb, you're a practical young man. Daddy was a man of his time. That's all."

"He crushed my hand. And he liked it."

"It was a knee-jerk reaction that doesn't justify this absurd line of questioning. He acted out of instinct."

"I want to know. I want you to tell me if it's true. Where is Tunisia?"

"With her grandparents."

"Alive?"

ELAINE VILAR MADRUGA

"Of course she's alive, Caleb! My God, these questions!"

"Did they hurt her? Did they have the trained dogs rape her?"

"No! Stop it. Are you trying to vex me with these questions? You never used to be so fantasy-prone."

"Did you know about it too? Did you know what Dad was doing before he became an important man—"

"The first step toward healing is controlling your emotions."

"—and you still had his kids? You still let him stick it in?"

"Caleb!"

"I always thought it was my fault—"

"Now what are you talking about?"

"—or Casandra's fault, or Calia's. Like, that we were freaks. Like how Casandra is in love with objects, and Calia doesn't talk but she's a genius, and me and the suicidal animals . . . all that stuff. But I was wrong."

"I don't understand you, Caleb. The first step toward healing is controlling your emotions and overcoming these harmful states of mind."

"At school we were always alone. And on the street, and at the zoo. Everyone stayed away. Because of Dad, no one wanted to be near us. It's his fault we've never had friends. Who'd want to be friends with a torturer's kids?"

"Don't you use that word!"

"I want to know."

"You want to know? Okay, I'll tell you. So, listen close and quit repeating all the lies the enemies of this nation tell. Can't you see the pain they've caused us? Can't you see what they did to your father after he gave this country years of unconditional service? It's unacceptable, Caleb. Your father did his duty. He was a hero in the service of history. Why should he apologize for that? Only he knows what he did and he has no trouble sleeping at night."

"And you? You don't have anything to apologize for?"

"Caleb, can't you see? Can't you see it's impossible for me to say I love you when you talk this way?"

"I hope Calia kills us all."

"Get out of here. Get out! The session is over."

"And I hope she kills the two of you first so Casandra and me can watch. I hope the butterflies fly up your nose and choke you."

"Get out of here, you little shit!"

"And I hope it's slow. I hope it's really, really slow."

Uh-huh. I admit I liked seeing Caleb's hand all bandaged up. I guess so, anyway. Honestly, I didn't have a lot of time to enjoy his swollen fingers, which proved my predictions were right and Caleb's pragmatic skepticism was wrong. Casandra syndrome, it's a curse. I get that my victory is a Pyrrhic one, but at least it pays homage to my namesake. I mean, it pays homage to the Trojan princess from whom I inherited both a name and an unhappy aptitude for making accurate predictions about the future that no one believes. Obviously, in my case, this isn't a divine gift or mythic superpower, I'm not trying to deify myself, okay? I just pay attention. If I'm good at anything in life, it's paying attention to other people's reactions, and my family, thanks to geographic and genetic proximity, has been a gold mine ripe for exploitation.

Successfully anticipating events is gratifying.

Cacasandra becomes Casandra, the Trojan princess, a name that suits me better and spares me the indignity of the fecal prefix.

I didn't know about Caleb's bandaged hand until hours after Dad crushed it with his boot. But I heard my little brother screaming. Pretty terrible, right? Even Calia, who is always indifferent to everything except her drawings, hasn't been able to finish her sketch of a monarch butterfly wing since hearing Caleb scream: the insect's former anatomical perfection has given way to a hack job of crisscrossed lines. Calia knows it, but she doesn't dare erase. It's a biological fact: the cries of a member of our same spaces trigger the fight-or-flight response.

To flee or not to flee, that's the question, Shakespeare.

In the interest of precision, or in the interest of realism, I should correct my earlier statement: Caleb didn't scream, he howled. And so did Dad. I don't know whose metamorphosis was worse, if it was the usually taciturn Caleb pleading, *Dad you're hurting me, Dad, please,* or if it was Dad rhythmically replying, *You won't laugh in my face next time, dissident. Next time, I'll rip off your fingernails and toenails, dissident.*

That image was so visceral I almost threw up.

All the world's a rage, Shakespeare.

Then the howling died down and silence took hold. If you think about it, that's even worse, because at least when someone's howling, you know where the pain—and the threat—is coming from.

I comforted myself by smelling my own skin. There was still something left there, my beloved's rusty aroma. If anything vanquishes death, it's sex. If anything vanquishes the howl of pain, it's the object of desire. The smell was beginning to fade and I hated myself because I was unable to retain my greatest love's fragrance.

When they write the history of frustration, they'll have to talk about Casandra, and they'll probably have to mention Caleb too. I'm not just waxing poetic, this is a real fact-based claim, okay? The day after the night of howling, I saw Caleb on the stairs. By which I mean we crossed paths, had an impromptu encounter, were thrown together by chance. I could see the tragedy in his eyes, the angel of death's lesser tragedy. Now that we're all in lockdown, he can't do anything except contemplate

ELAINE VILAR MADRUGA

his unfinished masterpiece. An angel of death turned sculptor with a bandaged hand. God knows who bandaged it. What did he have left? Basically nothing, just fantasies of better times when he'd be able to go outside, to the formerly unremarkable garden. Oh, of course, his lesser tragedy didn't hold a candle to my own personal drama, whose roots were much more visible and whose nature was irreversible, since my beloved is immobile. Some say true love waits, and this is especially true in our case, since the object of my desire must await the subject of her love. But let me ask if this is reason enough to forget the pain. Let me ask if there is any force strong enough to keep the subject of love, the only mobile party in the relationship, away from the object of her desire. Inflect those sentences like questions, or in a tone of desperate surprise, then reply: *Why, yes, there is such a force, and it's my father*. Let's not broaden the discussion, okay? Dad is the guilty party.

I didn't have to look into my brother's eyes twice to know what I had predicted weeks earlier—Caleb and I had a common enemy.

And that common enemy was the man with the medals, our father, the erstwhile stutterer transmogrifying into an ever-more-faithful facsimile of Pop-Pop Mustache.

A man with a stutter doesn't deserve his people's trust, but let the record show, neither does a man with a mustache.

In our tiny nation called home, the revolution had begun.

That cousin whose features were already beginning to fade was suddenly reborn. Desperate dreams. Caleb awoke with the claustrophobic sensation that there was not enough air in the house, that they were all trapped. What would happen if Dad decided consuming less air was an indispensable step toward the development of their nation-family, what would happen if Dad pointed his finger at the one superfluous head, the one that had to be eliminated so the shortage of air could become an abundance of air, with everyone else's approval and to everyone else's benefit?

In Caleb's dreams—that is, his nightmares—Tunisia was always escorted by German shepherds, rottweilers, Dobermans, dogs trained to track the scent of a female in heat, that is, the scent of any female, a useful skill when it came to raping the daughters of the enemies of the people. Over and over, Caleb had the same dream—that is, the same nightmare—with minor variations: Tunisia, escorted by the dogs, carrying a small bundle in her arms, a bundle that drew breath. Tunisia's chest—that is, her boobs—had become scrawny hides, nothing like the breasts Caleb fantasized about. He wished that were the worst part, but that was nothing compared to the bundle suckling at her breast, a baby with the head of a dog, sometimes a German shepherd, other times a rottweiler, Tunisia's mutant spawn in diapers cut from girls' blue, red, and fuchsia thongs. If anyone asked you how the mutant looked in Tunisia's arms, you would have to tell the truth: it looked comfortable, pleasantly swaddled. The creature that Tunisia was offering to Caleb with arms outstretched was almost tender; he isn't yours, but if you adopt him, he'll be a good son to you. He'll take care of the house and bring you your newspaper and slippers.

In the real world, the pain in his hand had started to wane, or at least, Caleb convinced himself it had. Nights were difficult. His swollen fingers throbbed and he repeated to himself, *Nothing is broken, it can't be, my hand is getting better*. He wished the pain were the worst part, but the worst part was Dad's nightly inspections.

Between three and five in the morning, Dad would get up and make coffee and the smell would slip under their doors, an olfactory omen of what was to come. They would have to get up. A few minutes later, they would hear the cry:

"Fall in!"

He would kick their doors with the soles of his boots.

"No war is won without sacrifice! No nation is forged except through fire!"

Once upon a time, Dad's voice had just been pointless noises on the other side of the door. Not anymore. His voice demanded obedience, and they opened their doors on command. Caleb was the first to comply. Then Casandra. Finally Calia, who came out with paper and pencils in hand, opening her eyes with a yawn.

"Loyalty! Heroism! Duty!" and then, "Attention!"

Dad was wearing his uniform, ironed to perfection. Occasionally, Mom would call out from another room: "Several studies have shown that sleep deprivation often leads to traumatic childhood afflictions."

"You too, dissident. Has your bad blood forgotten what a guerrilla march looks like? Get your heels and come," Dad commanded, and Mom's voice vanished. "Better dead than defeated! Better defeated than disloyal! Long live our homeland!"

It looked tragicomic. It was not. Casandra hazarded an ironic smile in protest. She was tired of standing at attention by her door, tired of Dad barking slogans between grunts.

"Blah dee blah, come on, it's four in the morning!"

Dad raised his whip.

When we say "whip," we mean whip. Not an imaginary or metaphorical whip, not the scourge of his lacerating threats, but a physical object, far more terrifying than Caleb's recurring dreams about Tunisia and the rapist dogs.

Casandra did not protest again.

"Roll call! Private Casandra, for love of country . . . !"

Roll call was a looming protocol to which they were to respond with a single word. The instructions had been sent in advance: they were to begin with the eldest and conclude with the youngest—that is, the boy with the bandaged hand was sandwiched between Casandra and Calia.

"Uh, yeah, here I guess," she said in the most insubordinate tone she could muster, but her voice betrayed her fear and even trembled a little.

"Private Caleb, for love of country . . . !"

"Here."

"Private Calia, for love of country . . . !"

"Calia doesn't talk, Dad," Caleb tried to defend his little sister, who had recently begun sucking on her pencils as if they were a nipple or a thumb.

"Private Calia, for love of country . . . !"

"She's here!" even the ever-ironic Casandra was indignant. "Look, she's obviously right there!"

"Private Calia, for love of country . . . !"

Brittle layers of frustration were settling into Dad's voice, shiny like ice about to shatter. We use the word "ice" with all the revolutionary implications it carries, because there is debate as to whether ice even exists or if it is another clever component of the enemy's propaganda, a word invented by the enemies of the people who are always scouring for stains on the nation, who, when they use the word "ice," surely aim to question the heat of our homeland and its endless summer.

"Private Calia, for love of country . . . !"

"She can't talk!" Caleb replied.

"Then she better learn fast," replied the man with the medals, crouching so his head was level with Calia's. "And she'd better trade those little pencils for something befitting of a soldier, a more dignified duty that suits a daughter of this great nation. Understood, Private Calia?"

In reply, the child sucked her pencil harder.

Caleb's nightmares got worse the following week, most likely due to the lack of sleep. They were required to do roll call three times a night, which did not leave much time for closing his eyes and remembering better days. In Caleb's latest nightmares, Tunisia was sucking her thumb, sucking a pencil, indiscriminately sucking the head of her mutant baby, and from afar, from the depths of his dream-abyss, Caleb could hear a noise, but he could not tell if it was a whip cracking in the air or a pencil cracking in a mouth.

C asandra slowly descended the stairs to the basement; it was one of the few places that, through some blessed miracle, Dad had yet to begin monitoring, perhaps because it was a place of no immediate concern. It held nothing but residue of the past: old photo albums, old books in boxes, old moth-eaten papers; not even Caleb had managed to catalogue that realm of reminiscences in its entirety. For the moment, he trusted that his work of art was safely outside his father's destructive reach. But he was not stupid. He knew that he was working against the clock and that the clock, in turn, was working against his masterpiece. If Dad found it, all Caleb's effort would have been in vain.

Every day was a challenge. Every day he was careful as he crept downstairs, God forbid Dad spot him, God forbid Dad punish him; sneaking to the basement in the wee hours of the morning was no easy task, but God forbid Dad kick his puzzle into oblivion or crush Caleb's other, healthy, surviving, as-yet unbandaged hand.

Despite the darkness of the basement, Caleb did not dare turn on the lights. He caressed his unfinished masterpiece and tried not to think about Tunisia. Meanwhile, under his fingers, he petted a squirrel's frail bones or a sparrow's dry feathers. The puzzle was not uniform and it was not meant to be. Art is a process, and that was especially true of Caleb's art, which was—and we say this without irony or knowing winks—a still life. Caleb probed the various stages of decomposition within his work.

That was when he heard Casandra's feet on the stairs.

Nightmare. The darkness changed the sound. Caleb imagined that noise marked the return of Dad's boots, marked the ineluctable discovery of his art in the only part of the nation-house where one could act with freedom, the only space where he felt comfortable with his calling as angel of death.

It was no secret: Casandra and Caleb were not friends.

They were siblings, true, but that was a genetic condition, a hereditary burden they could not unshoulder, a done deal they had no choice but to accept; they were blood of the same blood, sperm of the same sperm, and erstwhile users of the same uterus at different moments, each spending their requisite season in the maternal timeshare. First Casandra, then Caleb two years later.

For the first time in his life, Caleb was relieved to see his sister—or rather, her silhouette in the dark basement.

"Now are you ready to negotiate?" she asked with a tone of feigned innocence, though she had the good sense to avoid stating the obvious with comments like "I told you so" or "serves you right," which would have proved effective and were certainly true, but which Caleb would have found offensive.

"Uh, yeah, I guess," Caleb replied to the silhouette with the voice of his older sister. "I guess I have no choice, bridgefucker."

"*We* have no choice, bunnykiller."

"But how do we . . . ? Maybe it'd be better to wait until the end of summer, maybe he'll stop. Sometimes people just go crazy temporarily, right? That's what they say."

"You really think that's what's happening?"

Caleb thought about Tunisia and his nightmares of the mutant, dog-faced baby.

"Anyway, trust me, okay?" Casandra added. "I have experience with these things."

"What things?"

"Pop-Pop Mustache was an expert, like a teacher, okay? He taught me everything I need to know." She sighed. The walls have ears, all walls have ears, how does Caleb not understand that the walls have ears? Does he just not care? What the hell family did her brother come from? Had he been so busy ripping up bunny rabbits that he had not learned anything in all those years? "So just shut up and trust me."

"Why were you always so close with Pop-Pop Mustache?"

Questions, questions, questions. Boring fucking questions. Just as boring as Caleb. Casandra sighed again. She had resolved to be patient, but the best words she could summon were:

"Jesus Christ, in Shakespeare, forging alliances with idiots is so easy—come on, Cacaleb, don't make this harder than it has to be," she said, then added, "Pop-Pop Mustache loved me, okay? And sometimes I helped him out."

"Helped him out how?"

"Seriously? Curiosity killed the cat, okay?" she stepped closer to Caleb. "Ugh, fine. But this isn't happy-puppy-story-time, I'll make it quick: when our aunt and uncle did *what they did*, or when they tried to, I . . . warned him."

Caleb was so close to his big sister that he could smell her hair and armpits. That physical proximity, at other moments, would have made him nauseous. Now he just felt unease, something undefined extending from the vicinity of his crotch, pulsing and twinging with a life of its own. Memories of his sister's multi-

ELAINE VILAR MADRUGA

colored thong parade and Tunisia's slow-fading face. Again he smelled it, you might even call it inhuman, though sometimes, as everyone knows, words fail to reflect the fullness of the senses. When he came closer to his sister, Caleb tried to define that aroma, tried to memorize it, stamp it in his pituitary gland.

"You mean . . . Dad knew . . . *what they did*? He was working with . . . ?"

Caleb could not see his sister's face, but he could have sworn that, in the darkness, she was smiling.

"Okay, I admit maybe I just got lucky when I talked to Pop-Pop Mustache. I've always been good at gambling and that time I bet it all. But I want to make this clear: I don't regret it, Caleb. I said what I said. I lied, I didn't lie, who cares? All's well that ends well."

"Hmm . . ." Caleb suddenly could not think of anything to say. "So, it was you who . . . betrayed Dad?"

"I don't like that word."

"Don't fuck with me, Casandra. It's the only word that really fits to . . . to describe . . . *that*."

She shrugged and sniffed the air.

"Caleb, for the love of God, tell me that dead-bunny smell isn't an actual dead bunny. Tell me you killed anything except another bunny," she grumbled.

"No, it's a sparrow . . ."

Casandra made a sound of disgust. Though to be fair, in the darkness, every sound became an expression of either nausea or fear. Caleb paid no attention, because the senses take many forms and dance to many instruments, and at that moment, he was concerned only with the closeness of his sister, who, in the shadows, might as well have been Tunisia or any other girl.

"So it's a deal," Casandra concluded. "We have no choice. We'll destroy him."

"And her. Don't forget her."

"Mom?" Casandra asked. "Really? Okay. Fine by me. I thought the two of you got along. I thought you got along with her better than I do anyway."

"She always knew Dad was a fucking monster."

"Okay, as you like it," she shrugged. "Measure for measure."

"Do you think it's true . . . ? Do you think he could've . . . ?"

The question hovered in the air for a few seconds before Caleb tried to continue. He mumbled a few formless syllables, then fell silent.

"You wanna know if Dad did *things* for Pop-Pop Mustache? But not just any *things*, right? You wanna know if he was a—"

"A murderer . . . if he tortured people," he said, completing his sister's sentence.

"Yeah. Dunno. Dad climbed pretty high. And to climb high, you gotta be tough. Does it matter?"

"Tunisia . . . ," he whispered the name but said no more.

". . . Tunisia is very far away from here, it's true. So, you know. You and me are a couple of tragic heroes." Casandra laughed again. "Who would've guessed? We have something in common after all, Bunnykiller Caleb."

Humor me, Casandrita. I know you're getting too big now for this sort of foolishness. Look at you. So tall, you'll drive the boys crazy with those long legs. And such an ass already, you're a bona fide knockout! Now, come sit here on your Pop-Pop Mustache's old bones. Don't be scared. Come. They've taken a lot of life's pleasures away from me over the years, Casandrita, but I can still look. I can still smell. What do you smell like?"

"Eau de violet."

"Like heck you do! What fragrance is that?"

"Rust."

"Let's see, let me . . . why, it's true. How odd. Now, come here. Have a sniff. What do you smell?"

"Nothing."

"Exactly. That is the aroma of old age: pleasantly neutral. I admit, it's a relief in some ways. Do you have any guesses as to why?"

"It could be worse, I guess."

"Exactly! A knockout with a good head on her shoulders. I could smell like guilt, or blood, or power. Or like a decrepit old man who pisses and drools all over himself. Pleasantly neutral isn't so bad, all things considered. What does your father smell like, Casandrita? You know your Pop-Pop gets very curious."

"I dunno."

"But you know other things, don't you? I can see it in your eyes, you little stunner."

"My aunt and uncle came over to eat on the weekend. Dad was talking to them for a long time."

"You don't say . . ."

"In private."

"Where were they?"

"Dad's office, where he keeps his medals. We aren't allowed in there. No one is, except Dad and now my aunt and uncle. It's a holy place."

". . . a secret place, then. Have I mentioned that your aunt and uncle aren't exactly friends to your Pop-Pop Mustache? They might even want to hurt me."

"Does Dad want to hurt you?"

"Do you have to ask? Don't you already know the answer, Casandrita?"

"Are you gonna give me your chair?"

". . . the chair you love?"

"Yes."

"Strange how you would ruin your old man's career just for an office chair."

"I *love* that chair."

"I have loved things too, you know. Objects, ideas . . . what did your father talk about with your aunt and uncle?"

"I dunno, they were in his office. Hiding."

"Is that the right word? Hiding?"

"It's a holy place . . . that's all I know, okay? You wanted me to tell you the truth. So that's it."

"You're a good girl."

"I guess."

"It's clear, then. You father is likely an enemy of the people. He could even be an enemy of your family. An enemy of you, Casandrita. You did the right thing, telling your Pop-Pop Mustache."

"Are you gonna give me the chair or what?"

"I'm a man of my word."

"What will happen to Dad . . . ?"

"To your father? We'll see. You don't have to worry about that sort of thing. Not yet."

"Will he know I . . . ?"

"There's no need for theatrics, Casandra. This isn't a tragedy. Besides, you did your duty. You're a good girl. A heroine. Every great story needs a heroine, you know. So here you are. You sniffed out your father's secrets. That's no easy task, but it has its merits. It's a very complex mission, and one for which your country thanks you. Because you see, Casandra, secrets can be dangerous. Just like smells. You and I are different from other people, Casandra. With others, things aren't so simple. Not everyone smells like rust. Not everyone smells pleasantly neutral."

Dad was in charge of rationing the food. Once per week he ventured into the outside world and returned with the triumphant air of a conqueror. Passersby still recognized his face on the street, but he was gradually reverting to the anonymous silhouette of the man he had once been. Ingratitude and collective amnesia are an epidemic in this country, Dad was sure of it. Still, the prospect of being an ordinary citizen, of walking past his neighbors without being pointed at, was starting to bring some comfort. Before the fall from grace, he could never go outside without drawing attention. There was no privacy because he was a man of the people, a man with history on his back, an extraordinary burden that often goes unacknowledged. But now, what a joy. He no longer had to play the part, no longer had to tighten his chest so the medals looked their finest. Now he could hunch at the shoulders and waist—he had chronic lower back pain—and allow himself to feel old, allow himself to wear tennis shoes or even flip-flops if he wanted. The world was now a place of infinite possibility.

Never before had he done the grocery shopping. He had taken that task for granted every day of his life. It did not matter how the bread ended up on the table. It was simply there. The world of privilege he enjoyed thanks to General Mustache had regrettably come to an end. But this new reality was not so disappointing, it merely required more work: the effort of walking to the nearest shop, the effort of asking for a pound of meat and haggling over the weight, the effort of sooner or later encountering the men and women from his past who, like Dad, had gone to the same shop to haggle over the same pound of black-market meat. The only differences between them and Dad were the respective positions they used to occupy in the interrogation room (sitting or standing), their role in that room (asking questions or answering them), and their relationship to the cattle prods and trained dogs deployed there (ordering or enduring their use). This situation was far from perfect and, frankly, a bit uncomfortable. But Dad knew that a good soldier can acclimate to even the most challenging of duties, despite the effort and the haggling and the gazes of individuals who may or may not have been past acquaintances whom he had endeavored to erase from his memory.

The civilian world had its own rules. With which Dad was not familiar. He had no idea that in the state shop, customers lined up to purchase their food, or that every family was expected to bring their own ration book. He learned all this the hard way, through trial and error, without complaint. He just gritted his teeth and stretched out his toes in his new civilian shoes, which were bigger than military boots but which he could somehow never break in. He learned that old medals carried no weight in the checkout line, at least not when those medals belong to a possible enemy of the people. He was a practical man; he stopped wearing them. The medals were also a reminder of who he used to be. They gave him away. In his new civilian life, Dad wanted to be just a faceless man in line with other faceless men, waiting with their ration books.

An everyman.

At first, the hostility was more apparent. It was in the air. Dad did not need to be especially perceptive to notice the hate that had built up in layers, in serpentine scales of resentment, in those interminable lines where people vented their grievances as they waited for their ration of fish cakes, eggs, cookies, supplies for children younger than six. They all regarded Dad as an intruder, a man from another galaxy, from another realm, the realm of power, which common men could not understand on an intellectual level, but which they nevertheless feared.

They also feared Dad, or rather, what Dad represented, what he had been in the past. The *things* he had done.

Forgetting was not a simple, overnight process. Besides remembering a man with a stutter, those people may have also recalled a voice in the torment ward demanding addresses, names, other pieces of information that would reveal who was an enemy of the people and who was a friend. All the survivors said so: he's a man who draws out his syllables, wears medals on his chest, shouts. It was a vague description, but people's imaginations tend to run away with them. If anyone in the rations line had dared to ask him, how do you sleep at night, you dirty son of a bitch, Dad would have calmly replied, *I sleep on my side with two pillows under my head and my room and my soul as dark as a dungeon.* If anyone in the rations line had persisted and asked how the fuck can you live with yourself after what you did, Dad would have calmly replied, *What have I done besides serve my people and my General, besides defend this country's interests at any cost? I am a practical man, and I followed the orders I was given without hesitation. Tell me, are orders meant to be questioned? No, of course not, orders are meant to be followed. These are not the hands of a butcher.*

And Dad's hands were not, in fact, a butcher's. Dad's hands had never come into contact with blood or any other bodily fluids of questionable provenance, those fluids the body expels from every possible orifice in an evacuation akin to escape, because even if the body cannot flee, it will still try, and the bodies in the interrogation laboratory were determined to get out of there in any state of matter, be it liquid, solid, or gas. It did not matter because Dad had never touched a prisoner. In fact, he found the interrogation laboratory and its methods a bit nauseating, but he considered them a necessary evil. Orders were not meant to be questioned, and if he was presented with an enemy of the people, well, out with the enemy's fingernails, out with the enemy's teeth, cattle prod to the enemy's testicles; if the enemy was a woman, it was standard practice to forget she was a woman, as a rule she became an object, put a cigarette out on the enemy's tits, run a train on the enemy till she talks, yeah you like that, enemy, you like it hard, you tasty terrorist fuckmeat. Wailing was ubiquitous in the interrogation laboratory, but that did not get in the way of Dad's sleep. He would give the orders—*give the bastard another prod or else tatake him to the tatatanks to play sususubmarines*—then go to his office for a little catnap until someone knocked on his door with news. *The birdie's chirping* if they talked, *the birdie broke* if the torture had gone too far, or *the cunt won't talk* if it was a woman, because women were the worst. *Shove her head in her own shit and show the bibitch who's boboboboss*, Dad would sing. Then he would return to his nap until there was more news.

He was a practical man.

He slept soundly.

He had an excellent appetite.

So it was a shame that in Dad's new life, food was rationed.

As he waited his turn in those endless lines, a few gazes fell on him. At first it was with fear. Then they got used to him. The gazes turned incredulous. No way is that man—the one hunched over with back pain, the douchebag in fucking flip-flops—the same man we saw on television, the same nightmare described by survivors of the interrogation lab. Their eyes were playing tricks on them. They must be.

That particular morning, the outing had been quick and productive. Dad was content. The line had not been long and he had gotten hold of some eggs and even two bottles of milk; the bread did not look great, but nothing in this world is perfect, he consoled himself. He had just begun shuffling back home, taking the same route as always, whistling a tune, what a beautiful morning, so splendidly warm, when the woman stepped in front of him; there was something unspeakable in her eyes, something horrific.

"You don't remember me," she said, "but I remember you."

Dad tried to avoid eye contact, tried to continue on his way, but the woman jumped in front of him again.

"You sadistic son of a bitch."

"Excuse me," Dad mumbled. The syllables began to stumble over each other: "I dodododon't knoknow you. You're loolooloolooking for sosomeone else."

She let him continue walking, then began to follow two steps behind.

"Leleave me alone. I'll cacacall the authorities!"

A thick gob of saliva. On the sidewalk. Between Dad's feet.

On the second try, her aim was better. She concentrated, or she had been working on her marksmanship, and her warm, viscous spit bathed the big toe of Dad's left foot. Disgusting, crazy-eyed woman. Disgusting, mucousy drool sliding slowly across his foot.

He chose to ignore her.

"Neaneaneanderthal," he muttered.

He was certain of it: she was one of those cunts, one of those birdies who would not sing even if they were plunged in shit up to their throat. If, at that moment, Dad had had a cattle prod, if Dad had had a porta-potty in which to submerge this dissident birdie's head, he would not have hesitated for so much as a second.

He walked the rest of the way home in fear.

The sensation of fear was horrible.

The woman had not followed him. Dad watched the street closely, scrutinized every face that walked past, made arbitrary turns left and right, took a new route home, all so the crazy-eyed, loogie-flinging birdie could not find him. But he was unable to banish the uncertainty from his head. The uncertainty was terrible. What if the birdie knew his whereabouts? What if the birdie was more than a mere flinger of harmless loogies? What if he encountered her in the park, or on the sidewalk, or in front of his house, or in the long line for rationed food? What if, instead of spitting on his feet, she spit in his eye? What if, instead of spitting in his eye, she shot him in the face?

Dad tried to open the door. His hand was trembling. He could not find his keys.

It was Caleb who eventually heard his father and opened the door.

"There are enemies everywhere," Dad said as soon as he crossed the protective threshold. "Human animals."

Caleb shrugged. "Did you get cookies?" he asked.

It was an inoffensive question, but Dad got an itch in the palm of his hand. "Is that all you got to say, little birdie?"

"It's okay. I didn't want cookies anyway."

Caleb managed to dodge the hand in time. Dad marched to the center of the living room and took off his flip-flops. The trail of saliva had settled between toes. It glistened.

"Where is Casandra?" Dad demanded.

"In her room," Caleb replied.

So birdie bridgefucker was out of his reach. Dad was not capable of climbing the staircase, especially with his lower back pain. Nor did he care to get into a shouting match with Caca-sandra and her dramatic way of speaking. Bridgefucker bitch. He looked at Caleb, took account of his grievances. Someone had to pay for the hot gob squishing under the base of his big toe, it did not matter who, it could be the woman in the street, but it could just as well be any of the bastard birdies who lived in his house, blood of his blood, like this cookie-gobbling birdie in front of him, for example.

With firm steps, he approached Caleb.

"Come here," he hissed, but the boy backed away.

"No."

"Come here, now. That's an order."

Blind with rage, Dad did not see where he was stepping.

In the middle of the living room, Calia sat among crayons, pencils, paintbrushes.

Dad tripped over the girl, spilling watercolors on the sheets covered in monarch butterflies. Even worse, one of his feet—

incidentally the same one that had been defiled by that woman and her yellow-tinged saliva—stepped on the sharpened tip of a pencil.

It barely hurt, but it was enough.

Enough for him to grab Calia by the hair and shout in her ear.

"Sing for me, you worthless birdie bitch, or I'll break your fucking beak!"

And Calia did sing, in her way, a song that came out as a howl, and Dad tugged harder on her hair, pulled so hard the follicles seemed about to detach from her cranium.

"There are pencils all over the place, you stupid cunt! I'm gonna dunk your head in the toilet and take a dump on your idiot fucking face!"

Over and over: birdie bitch, bitch birdie.

Caleb tried to retreat but tripped on the stairs. He wanted to go up to his room, to lock the door and forget about all of this, but Calia's howling was anything but birdsong. The child who had never spoken a word, who had never taken the least interest in the world around her, looked like a plastic doll about to snap. From somewhere, from everywhere, new cries began to sound, hers, Casandra's, someone's, blending with the howls of the girl with the crayons, the girl with the butterflies, and it would have been perfect if, at just that moment, Calia had spoken, as Mom had prophesied, or if the butterflies had risen from the white page and rescued their creator, if they descended like an apocalyptic swarm on Dad, if piranhic butterflies had nibbled that wannabe tyrant motherfucker down to the bone, if God had taken hold of Calia's voice and bellowed a call for destruction, a global flood, a pandemic, a *now our death begins*. Such a miraculous denouement would have released Calia from Dad's clutches, but those things do not happen, not in novels and not in real life. We have to say it: the butterflies remained lifeless on the page, flat and artificial, God did not speak and neither did Calia, though howling is a dead language that, unfortunately, all of us still understand.

CALIA

Butts on monkeys. Antennae on ants. Eyes on spiders. Spindly hairs on elephant trunks. Fractal patterns on butterfly wings.

On the surface of her cranium, in that valley of death that produces nothing but thoughts and hairs, there is a terrible burning heat. The cranium is a weak and sacred dwelling place. Who is profaning the urn where Calia rests and paints? Who is desecrating this graveyard? The reaction is logical, the reaction is animal, a law of the biological world. As the hand tightens its grip, the pain grows greater. As the pain grows greater, the cries grow louder and quickly become howls.

It hurts the same when they brush her hair, when they try to brush her hair. Correction: it does not hurt the same. The sensation is not pleasant; it stings her cranium. The bristles of the brush do not have permission to dig into Calia's sacred dwelling place, but at least hatred is not in the air, she cannot smell dry phlegm, she certainly cannot smell shouting.

Butts on monkeys. Antennae on ants. Eyes on spiders. Spindly hairs on elephant trunks. Fractal patterns on butterfly wings.

Between howls, Calia notices small details: her forehead sweating, her head burning, the stairway leading somewhere, the temperature in the room increasing; that is why the flies are everywhere. The flies are intelligent animals and they govern all things living and dead in their own fashion. There is no place on this earth that the flies do not control, no skin, no surface, no nature. The tyranny of flies is a life philosophy that Calia has learned all too well, which is why she lets them land wherever they like, on her blank and not-blank papers, on the sketches from her elephant period or her monkey-butt period or her monarch butterfly period.

In fact, the flies land on Calia's howls and she lets them; acclimating to their tyranny is essential. Calia is the most intelligent member of the family. She knows the flies appreciate the effort she makes to not brush them away, even though they tickle her and their little legs track muck all over her skin as they march up and down her pores. Calia is not like the others, she is not like the man who is shaking her, for example. The man who is shaking her hates the flies, he shoos them off his hands, his chest, especially his face. They bother him most when they land on his face. The man who is shaking Calia cannot bear any tyranny but his own. It may not seem like it at first, but the flies know about him, they know he cannot stand them, they smell it and they feel it, which explains why the man currently shaking Calia is the dumping ground for load after load of fly shit. The flies can be vengeful, persistent little fuckers when they put their mind to it.

Butts on monkeys. Antennae on ants. Eyes on spiders. Spindly hairs on elephant trunks. Fractal patterns on butterfly wings.

How long have we been married . . . ?"

"An eternity."

"But how long exactly . . . ?"

"I don't know. How old is Casandra? A little longer than that."

"And you've never been honest with me."

"What does that have to do with how old Casandra is?"

"You've never told me the truth."

"No . . . but I bought you shoes. With heels. That's what you wanted at first. You asked for them all the time. Didn't you like them?"

"Now I want to know. When we met, you worked in that lab . . ."

"A laboratory of questions, yes, and answers."

"What did you do in there?"

"I followed orders, as always. I was a soldier. A soldier is a soldier wherever he goes."

"Even here? Even at home?"

"Correct."

"Even when we were making love?"

"Correct. That's what you wanted to know? That's all?"

"More or less."

"Curiosity is not more. Curiosity is not less. Curiosity is vile, unspeakable, unpatriotic."

"I've heard things."

"You don't say."

"Did you ever hurt anyone?"

"That's an ambiguous question. Take it from me, I know all about questions and answers, ambiguous and otherwise. I know about every sort of question and every sort of answer. I've heard plenty."

"You heard them in your . . . in the lab?"

"And in life."

"What did you do to your prisoners?"

"Prisoners is also an ambiguous word. Have you forgotten? The preferred term is 'enemies of the people.' Anyway, lower your voice . . . the children . . ."

"The children are asleep. They sleep like angels."

"Sleeping like an angel is a virtue."

"Was there anything virtuous about what you did at that laboratory?"

"What do you think? Look at these hands. Do you see them?"

"Yes."

"Do you see any darkness in them?"

"Lower your voice . . . the children . . ."

"The children will be proud of their father one day. Everything I did, I did for you. For you and them. And for your shoes."

". . . for my shoes?"

"You're a woman who likes tall shoes and big dreams. I've given you both. So shut up. You're worried about nothing. Think about your new set of heels."

"But . . ."

"No buts. Do you have flies for brains?"

"I want red ones, then."

"Red heels?"

"Stilettos. With black soles. They're elegant."

"Look how we understand one another. We're a good couple. A model of marital bliss. We have no reason to talk about laboratories. No reason to talk about enemies of the people. Bed is for sleeping and screwing, not for asking stupid questions."

Mom's heels echo throughout the house. She has begun wearing them all the time, even first thing in the morning and when she goes to the bathroom. The children have not seen her in a long time, but they are intimately familiar with the sound of her footsteps. Shoes going up and down stairs is the only sound in the house. Repetition and monotony. It is the closest thing to solitude. Casandra, Caleb, and Calia are still in their bedrooms. Restriction. And what is restriction but a set of rules that have been placed there, in the doors, where they have a supernatural effect akin to that of garlic upon vampires? Nobody ever goes in and nobody ever comes out. In fact, Dad has not even locked the doors. He knows he does not need to. Restrictions and locks are unnecessary if the children can be kept inside, isolated, taking refuge in the cage of their bedrooms with another supernatural element: fear.

In that house, everyone's breath has its own sound. The children have learned to identify the cadence of Dad sneezing, the timbre of Mom yawning. Their senses have sharpened. Now their noses are keener, their ears more attuned. Any vibration in the floor wakes them up. It could be Mom's heels or Dad's boots, or the announcement of roll call, or the moment the lights in their rooms are turned on. Sleeping this way is difficult. There is no day, there is no night, there is merely a progression of breaths: Casandra's is heavy, as if she lacks air;

Calia's is almost imperceptible, more of a whisper slipping through fingers; Caleb's is unintelligible; Mom's is a stiletto through the throat; Dad's is a whimper, a military march, a fearful exhalation.

In recent days, the children have noticed even the flies' breath. They seem to drone the song of a madman, one which Casandra, Caleb, and Calia hum together, a melody they have learned as a chorus.

The flies have sworn revenge.

Nothing will go unpunished under their many watchful eyes.

The hand that was raised against Calia's hair will not go unpunished. The hand that crumpled the sheets of butterflies will not go unpunished. The foot that crushed Caleb's fingers will not go unpunished. The voice that spent years asking useless questions, analyzing the children as if they were parasites in a laboratory, will not go unpunished. The human species, or rather, the inhuman species that occupies this house will not go unpunished. The flies drone on and the children believe their promises, arm themselves with patience, wait in a darkness that is not day and is not night.

At any given moment, Dad might get up. Turn on the lights. Summon them to the hallway in their underwear. Calia in a pom-pom bloomer that looks more like a diaper. She has pissed herself. Or shit herself. The air is redolent of shit, of teeth unbrushed for weeks. Casandra in her multicolor thongs. Caleb, so skinny his bones jut out over his briefs, is like a jigsaw puzzle, like the work of art he is building with the remains of dead animals. Dad looks at them. Casandra yawns. That is a mistake. His fist connects with her ribs. She doubles over. The flies sing their song, and the song urges the children to be patient. Nothing will go unpunished, but biding your time, awaiting reprisal, is not easy.

Dad asks the routine questions. Questions that are unnecessary because they are always the same. Mom's heels click across the kitchen. She remains, as always, on the fringes of conflict, because in this nation-house, Mom knows much and says little. It is what she has always done before and what she does now.

The children only see one another when summoned to the hall.

Casandra looks at Caleb, and both regard small Calia, somehow even smaller now, as if she has shrunk in the past few hours, as if she has ceased to grow. Calia does not return their gazes, because she lives immersed in her own world. Dad issues a new order. The children return to their bedrooms. Outside, the day is beginning to break, but for Casandra, Caleb, and Calia, night persists; they are sleepy and they sleep, it is the blankest night, a night where nothing exists but the desire not to.

The flies' promise of revenge is all that keeps the children attentive, with ears pressed against the unlocked doors.

Outside, Dad paces, barks orders at invisible soldiers, interrogates invisible prisoners, spits. There is no sound louder than spit striking a hardwood floor.

"You better start singing, little birdies. I said shut your mouth, bitch!" he cries at no one.

And then, when we all think he has finally fallen silent:

"That's it, right between her eyes."

n a quiet, convoluted kind of way, Calia is this novel's heroine too. She doesn't talk, but all it takes is one look and you can see how much she despises everyone and everything, though Dad's tireless efforts have put him at the top of her hierarchical shit list.

I will never forget the moment Calia's contempt for Dad took physical form. Just that morning, I had finally found a place in this domestic prison that was private enough to masturbate. I'm talking, specifically and predictably, about the day Dad practically pulled Calia's hair out of her skull, a day I have decided to call—in the seclusion of this bedroom-cage and always in a low voice because the walls have ears— "The morning of the hairsplitting howls."

We know how the drama started. Calia was reborn from the ashes of a half-bald phoenix. Dad had pulled out a few locks of hair, but we still expected her to do something breathtaking, even in her defeathered state. Mom crept up and watched from the hall, her eyes as anxious as ever, thrilled or terrified— at this point in the play, it's difficult to determine Mom's true motivations—by the miracle Calia was about to work.

I'm not talking about some grotesque, garden-variety miracle like multiplying loaves and fishes or transmuting copper into gold, I'm talking about *the* miracle of the butterflies. In other words, we were all expecting Calia to fulfill the family lore, to release her monarch butterflies from the page on which they had been created. If nothing else, we were expecting her to speak with the voice of God, a voice I've always imagined sounds like Pop-Pop Mustache's.

After that, the prophecy would continue to run its course, okay? A swarm of monarch butterflies would lift us into the air, sort of like a heavenly host but with more colorful wings. And then after that, I don't know, we would look death in the eyes or something. Death would be like a big fat butterfly that would hand down its verdict. In the weighing and measuring of humanity, the good would ascend into blah dee blah and the wicked would be cast down into blah dee blah, whatever, just pretend I said something concise, pithy, poetic. The point is we would all die. It would almost be like the end of a Shakespearean tragedy: *O happy butterfly, this is thy sheath*. I'd been practicing my final line and even rehearsing a few nostalgic gazes toward the horizon, where, not so far away, my immobile beloved was waiting.

But I guess that was asking too much. Dreams never come true, that's the law. Not even family lore. Not even the notions of collective death our mother has instilled in us from our first days on Earth. Calia's butterflies stayed on the page and she kept howling, and if anything was fluttering above our heads, it was just the flies. They're the real masters of this country, after all. Why'd we expect any different?

For the record, it was a letdown.

Uh-huh. The morning of the howls ended just as suddenly as it began. Dad let go of Calia, or I mean, he let go of Calia's hair, but a fistful stayed in his hand, like a trophy, looking anachronistic. Calia sat back down on the floor, grabbed a blank sheet of paper, and crawled around until she found a pencil or a crayon. And then she went back to drawing, like the morning of the hairsplitting howls never even happened.

Dad didn't have to give any new orders. I went to my room, lay on the bed, and closed my eyes. I tried to think about my beloved. I tried to touch myself and smell any trace of rust on my skin, but her fragrance faded more with each passing day. There I was, heroic, tragic, flavorless, with no aroma but my own—a crass, common Casandra, without hope for death or life, without any chance of leaving the house, without a sister capable of channeling the voice of God or even conjuring homicidal butterflies.

But everyone knows Calia has never been one for convention. Her heroine's journey wasn't going to be formulaic, and it definitely wasn't going to be obvious.

Here's how it went down.

The morning of the hairsplitting howls was fading from my memory. Calia kept drawing like always, nothing out of the ordinary. Sitting on the floor, with colors and crayon and pencils and pens scattered all around. She was still a baby savant, but no longer a supernatural one. She had been demoted from the category of the divine. Uh-huh. Usually, she doesn't do much that interests me. She just sits there. That's all. Sometimes we exchange a look of hatred or apathy, probably apathy, or at least something like it. The world of white drawing paper is her paradise, or maybe you could call it an immaculate prison she can't or doesn't want to escape from. That day I peeked over her shoulder, mainly because I wanted to see if the hairs Dad had ripped off her scalp looked like a priest's tonsure or some other kind of ritualistically shaved bald spot. I was just curious. My

sister's cranium was smooth and unblemished. Then I glanced at her drawings, her gorgeous monarch butterflies. I figured, now that I know my sister isn't a miracle worker or the voice of God, maybe I can swipe a few of her drawings, because honestly, she's really good. I thought that, as wall art, her butterflies might brighten up the darkness of my room and help me forget my own anodyne fragrancelessness.

"Lemme look, Calia . . . ," I said. Trying to talk to someone who doesn't want to reply is a bad habit, but whatever, some protocols are inviolable.

I looked at her papers, but they weren't blank.

They weren't covered in butterflies.

They weren't covered in elephants or spiders or bulbous monkey butts.

Her sketches were still anatomically precise. More than ever.

The papers were covered in flies. Uh-huh. They looked like they were practically crawling. Calia traced a wing, the little suction-cup legs, then looked up at me.

She was silent, but another sound occupied the room. It was coming from the paper.

The fly Calia had just finished drawing shook a drip of ink from its wings and took flight.

They sat at the table. The food was disgusting. Dad's cooking. Dad had never cooked in his life, but now he was in charge of everything, now he decided whether or not there was food, and now he calculated everyone's portions according to that day's behavior.

"We have to be frugal. Scarcity is an exercise in patience," he hissed in front of his empty plate, "and a good life lesson."

Mom was the only member of the family with food on her plate: an off-looking vegetable of unknown origin that she nevertheless ingested quickly and without complaint.

No one thought about whether the food was good or bad; their hunger had reached the point of desperation. Seeing Mom's mouth, which opened and closed on that formless vegetable, made their stomachs groan. For the second day in a row, Casandra, Caleb, and Calia had nothing to eat.

Calia had begun to lick and chew her crayons. Her mouth was always colorful.

"I'm hungry, Dad," said Casandra in a faint voice. Her face was beginning to take on the contours of her skull.

Dad looked up and pointed to his own plate.

"I am too, but I don't complain."

Caleb felt the urge to jump onto the table, empty fork in hand, empty plate in hand, and nestle the fork into Dad's head, shatter the plate on his scalp. The image vanished immediately. He sighed and concentrated on Mom's mouth, on her unhurried, formless way of swallowing, on the steadily vanishing vegetable. Caleb imagined for a second that he was her, that he was Mom. He could practically feel the egregious pain from those heels, his toes crushed together, the relief of food sliding down his digestive tract. It did not matter if it was a vegetable or raw meat. He held his breath.

"I still smell rot." Dad's hisses were serpentine. "I smell it everywhere in the house."

He swirled his mustache and brought an empty fork to his mouth.

"Thinking about food can be just as satisfying as chewing it," he said a moment later. "Don't you think, Casandra?"

"I guess."

"Do you know where that smell is coming from?" At first the question floated in the air, seemingly aimed at no one in particular, but eventually his eyes fell on the mouth chewing the amorphous vegetable.

"No," Mom lied. She did not give away the unfinished masterpiece.

". . . dead animals," Dad continued, "carry disease."

"It must be a rat or a squirrel or something small like that. The smell is practically gone now anyway," Caleb said, eagerly bringing an empty fork to his mouth.

"That's very nice, Caleb," Dad said, rewarding his son with a smile. "That's right, good boy. Now, don't you think your father is the best chef in the world?"

He did not wait for Caleb to reply. Instead, he thwacked a

spoonful of something onto the boy's plate, something resembling beet salad. Caleb's obedience had paid off. Whatever it was, he pounced on it like a dog onto a bare bone, tearing it apart before the hungry gaze of Casandra and Calia, and even of his father.

P op-Pop Mustache . . . ? Is Dad an important man?"

"What an interesting question, Casandrita."

"If he works for you, he has to be important because everyone is afraid of you."

"Afraid of me? Do you really think so?"

"I'm not though."

"No, of course not you. Why would you be afraid of me? I bring you dolls."

"But are people scared of Dad too?"

"That's a tricky question, Casandrita. It depends. Fear is tricky too."

"I don't get it."

"Well, let's see. Are you scared of your father?"

"No. I dunno. Sometimes."

"Why?"

"He always gets home late. What does he do at work?"

"Ah, that's another interesting question."

"Every time you say, 'that's an interesting question,' you don't answer."

"Do I not? I hadn't realized . . . you want to know what he does at work? Well, your father works in a tunnel. It's similar to a tunnel, anyway: it's dark in there, but it's also comfortable, at least for your father, and he has a big office there with a chair and a desk covered in papers, and they bring him three meals a day, plus two snacks. He spends the whole day signing papers and sometimes he walks through the tunnel. Did I mention there are little houses in the tunnel?"

"No."

"Ah, well, there are little houses in the tunnel. Little ant houses full of people."

"Are they ant houses or people houses?"

"People houses, of course. Ants are very disciplined creatures; they would never let themselves be locked up in a place like that."

"So, Dad takes care of those people?"

"Sometimes he takes care of them, other times he punishes them, or scares them, or breaks them . . . it depends, Casandrita."

"Why does he scare them?"

"Ah, that's another interesting question."

"I bet they get scared because he yells at them."

"Exactly. He yells at them a little, reprimands them. I'm sure you're familiar with your father's reprimands."

"No. Dad doesn't punish me."

"That's because you're a good girl, an obedient little worker ant. But those people, in those tunnels . . . sometimes they need to be subdued. They haven't learned. So your father has to teach them."

"So it's like a school."

". . . yes, exactly. A school for disciplining ants."

"Dad doesn't like ants."

"Imagine how hard it must be for the poor man, then! No one ever said it's an easy job."

"If they ask, can I say Dad is a teacher?"

"A teacher for ants? No, better to say something else."

"Like what?"

"I'm not sure. Perhaps that your father is a . . . truth seeker. Let's stick to that."

"What?"

"We have to get to the truth, no matter what it costs."

"I don't get it."

"You needn't get it, Casandrita."

"Pop-Pop Mustache . . . ?"

"Let me guess—you have another question."

"In those tunnels where people live . . . the bad people . . . is there sun in there?"

"Why, my darling Casandrita, they're under the earth. There is no sun underground."

"So how do they see?"

"They get used to it. The human eye can adapt remarkably well to darkness. Not to mention, fear is the sixth sense."

"The sixth what . . . ?"

"Touch, taste, sight, smell, hearing . . . and fear. Didn't you know?"

"No."

"There is no sun down there, Casandrita, but they don't need it. See? You've learned something new. Are you proud of your father?"

"I guess so."

t takes a real woman to pull off red stilettos. Screw your sensible heels. You have got to grin and bear it. Stilettos are for saints and subversives, nothing in between. It takes ovaries of steel to endure the crushed toes, the corns and calluses and ingrown toenails. It takes a real woman to ignore the pain shooting into her cranium and laying eggs in her brain like a big fat housefly.

Either you walk with pride, or you do not walk at all.

In the jigsaw puzzle that was the family, Mom felt out of place. The others all fit together, in one way or another. Their mutual hatred mobilized them, forced them into a common bond, however negligible. Hatred was the foundation holding the house up, but Mom had nothing but a single, sad cinder block of paltry resentments—resentments that the rest of the family would not even deign to reciprocate. She knew that to them, she would never be more than an egg-laying hen in red stilettos, too marginal to merit their scorn.

She sat across from Calia and plucked the crayons out of her daughter's mouth.

"Stop eating those and listen to me."

The girl glanced up as if surprised by a sudden noise, then proceeded to reach for another crayon, place it in her mouth, and resume gnawing. Mom insisted:

"Stop that, now. I know it's you. Under Calia's skin, I know you're there. I recognize you."

She was waiting for some sort of reaction, an expression, a smile to betoken the truth: the shadow of her aunt or the voice of God resided somewhere in the depths of that mute mouth. Everything that happened in the world had a purpose, did it not? Mom no longer understood, she had suddenly become elderly. She had always feared the arrival of the butterflies, but now they had vanished, leaving no footprints of God's call, no trail of destruction in their wake, and she felt only emptiness and hunger, the lonely failure of the last runner on the track after all the others have crossed the finish line.

"Calia, come on, do it. Do it already," she whispered to the hungry, mute, Crayola-gnawing child. "Why are you doing this to me? Why are you making me wait? Help me. I deserve it, don't I? Please, set me free. Where are the butterflies?"

Mom did not want to die. Mom did not want to keep living. Above all, Mom needed a purpose.

The waxy crayon paste disappeared behind Calia's teeth. The child did not look up. Mom went down to the basement.

ELAINE VILAR MADRUGA

Hello, Casandra. I'm glad you're back."

"I never left. I've just been in the other room, on the other side of this wall."

"It's a figure of speech, Casandra. You've always been prone to such literal patterns of thought."

"Okay, sure, I'm prone to literal patterns of fa-la-la."

"What would you like to talk about today?"

"You."

"Me?"

"Or Calia's butterflies. The ones that didn't fly off the page."

"A miscalculation."

"Or missed destiny. I always thought you were batshit. You told those stories, you know, about the butterflies and God and blah dee blah and fa-la-la. I always knew you were fucked in the head."

"Have you noticed that whenever you become passive, you also become rather aggressive? It's a textbook psychopathic tendency."

"Okay dunno uh-huh fa-la-la super blah dee blah."

"I don't imagine you came to this session just so you could say 'blah dee blah' at me."

"You know what's weird is, like, you have nothing in life except a pretty pair of shoes. I'm not an expert or anything, but you've wasted a lot of time. You weren't bad looking. But there's none of that left. You look like a mama rat that just gave birth to a litter of baby rats. Or, no! You know what you look like? A fly. You have resting fly face."

"Would you like to discuss your sexual paraphilias, Casandra?"

"No, thanks, my sexual para-fa-la-las and me are super. Sometimes I wonder though, like seriously, how long has it been since the last time you came, Mom? It's gotta be millennia at this point. Or, what do I know, maybe you've never had an orgasm at all. Is that why you're obsessed with analyzing everyone else's sexual para-fa-la-las, so you don't have to think about how you never come? Thank God for therapy. You must find it very helpful."

"Have you given that bridge of yours a name?"

"A bridge by any other name would smell as sweet, okay? Look, I don't know anything about life, but with that fly face, there's nothing else for you to do. You're fucked. You're a pathetic, totally fucked creature, Mom. You're a bug. I always wondered if bugs had orgasms."

"Do you always hyperfocus on sexual gratification with such intensity, Casandra? Do you think a happy life is all about orgasms? Why is that?"

"Totally. Orgasms are what freedom is all about. It's not something you can understand, you're too hyperfocused on your blahblahphilia. But I guess I should expect as much from a bug."

"Are you aware that scorn for one or both parents is an unconscious, not-so-subtle expression of the scorn an individual feels for herself, Casandra?"

"I don't know if you really are batshit, or if what you told us about your aunt and the butterflies was true, but honestly, I totally get why your family decided to leave you behind instead of letting you die with them. Living with you sucks . . . no, wait, I'll say it in blah-blah speak . . . sharing space with you is an opportunity to practice setting boundaries."

"What makes you say that, Casandra?"

"Like, look, like I said, I don't know anything about life, but if you're old, or basically old, and basically fly faced, and the only thing you have going for you is a pair of stilettos . . . like, I'm no expert, but Mom, you're a fucking failure."

"What makes you say that, Casandra?"

"The butterflies didn't pick you, Dad . . . for him you're less important than a drawer full of stamped metal. Calia'd rather chew crayons than look at you. And I think you're a fly."

"But Caleb . . . ?"

"Caleb? He wants to murder you. Or I mean, whatever, what do I know, he probably wants something more complicated than just murder. That kid's a hormone smoothie, he talks a lot of shit but I doubt he'll end up doing anything to you. But the desire is there . . . oh, Mom. What a waste."

"You're a monster, Casandra."

"It's just a waste. Why wait for the butterflies to kill you when you can do it yourself? Like, you don't need a pretext."

"You're a fucking monster."

"Uh-huh, monsters and medals and heels, oh my. Try and listen, Flyface. Try and think about other options, please. Try using your brain for once. There are some perfectly clean, hygienic methods. Or maybe not hygienic, I guess I'm not an expert, but anyway, there are methods. And they don't all involve wings. You don't need Calia. Take a little initiative. You can do this yourself and you can do this *for* yourself. Okay? You can disappear. When you think about it that way, the butterflies are just a means to an end."

The basement was damp, a space where the vapors of claustrophobia and incarceration had calcified. Mom felt incapable of taking another step. Fucking feet. Fucking toes. Fucking beautiful red stilettos with black fucking soles. Fucking floral dress. All of it rapidly soaking up the basement's stench, the bittersweet stink of decay. Not a step, not a single step farther, she still had time to change her mind, to fly far from that basement, far from Caleb's puzzle, maybe there is something she does not understand, maybe she does not belong down here with this art. But the flies all around her, what do they say, they merely invite, insist, entice, bat their wings and accompany her: *You're not alone, Mom, don't worry, Mom, it's us, it's the flies, it's your family, we flew here just to tell you that everything is going to be okay, you just go ahead, go down to the basement, don't even think about taking off those beautiful shoes, if you take off your shoes you'll get cold feet, Mom, it takes a real woman to stay strong to the bitter end, Mom, are you a fly or are you not, Mom, tell us.* And Mom continues down the stairs, escorted by gossamer wings, flanked by flies in their multitudes, and it is only now that she notices their existence, realizes where this swarm came from, because, in the house, there have always been bugs; flies are nothing new, but it has never been like this, they have never been so populous, so intelligent. In the past, they did not buzz with such music, are you a fly or are you not, a synchronous symphony of wings, a lullaby, rockabye, Mommy, what is the use, when the wind blows, you'll swing from your noose.

The insects land on Mom's floral dress, on her red stilettos, on her skin, they tunnel in her hair. She becomes a dwelling place, a fairground, a home to tyrants. She goes the rest of the way downstairs. There sits the unfinished masterpiece, the altar to decay on which the flies feed. This is where the animal corpses, Caleb's tributes, lie in eternal rest or eternal activity, because no one ever said that in death there is no movement. The flies buzz, the flies agree, we are not butterflies, but our nation is a place of celebration, our wings do not torture in vain, everything has a purpose and that purpose is you. Before the altar, Mom stops, sneezes. The basement is full of dust and debris, crumbs of a crumbling nation. That basement could be the history of the country or of the family, but that sort of reflection, however astute, no longer matters.

The flies buzz and Mom obeys, she searches, finds the rope, consigned to a corner in a mess of meaningless boxes and bundles. The rope becomes a knot. Mom is not good with knots, but the flies cheer her on, you can do it, just a simple knot, pull on that end of the rope, that's it, now straight to the support beam, chair underneath, that's right. Mom moves decisively, with a rigor not yet mortis, the rigor of fear, what if she fails at this too, what if she fails at her life's final purpose, what if she fails to cross the threshold and follow the flies down the rabbit hole. Being a failure has never been easy. Being a failure is traumatic. What if she's bad at tying knots, what if the rope is too long, what if it hurts, but the flies buzz peace in her ears, ease her worries, you know it takes ovaries of steel to kill yourself, Mom, you know it takes ovaries of steel to climb onto a chair in your stilettos, ignoring the corns and calluses and ingrown toe-nails, it takes ovaries of steel to jump without letting those shoes slip off, right there in front of the monument, the altar to the flies. It takes ovaries of steel to teeter from side to side like a mother hen, grab the rope *cluck cluck*, wrap it round your neck *cluck cluck*, draw your final breath *cluck cluck*, hop off the chair *cluck cluck*, and Mom gasps and dangles and writhes and, as she feels the darkness closing in, a sensation starts to coalesce be-tween her legs, a radiance that rises through her body and seizes her mind, emerging from oblivion and exploding in infinite cre-scendo, not the ephemeral, cresting climax of the living but the unrelenting release of la petite mort, and then her body sways *cluck cluck*, slow and inert *cluck cluck*, left and right *cluck cluck*, back and forth *cluck cluck*.

For every fly in the house, the banquet has begun. Acting of one accord, they blanket Mom in an operation akin to poetry or madness. They swarm in concert, caravanning across her red stilettos or loafing lazily on her blackening tongue, then begin the expedition through her mouth and down her throat.

've always liked the color black, so I had no trouble finding something to wear when I rifled through the clothes hanging in Mom's wardrobe. Hanging just like Mom! That's tragic irony for you. I picked a dress, the prettiest one: it was lacy and black and matched my hair and eyes perfectly. I'd always wanted that dress. The fit was almost perfect. When I put it on, it was like slipping into Mom's skin. And the timing couldn't have been better because he saw me, Dad saw me, and there was no emotion in his voice when he said:

"You look just like your mother." An oft-repeated phrase to which I could only respond with a touch of condescension and a smile I didn't even pretend was genuine.

He's a sick son of a bitch, okay? I haven't forgotten. Dad is a sick son of a bitch, which makes all of us the sick grandchildren of a bitch. Even if he's stopped using the fecal prefix and no longer stutters, there are things I can't erase, things I can't get out of my head. I guess it all comes down to revenge and personal satisfaction.

He was the one who went to the basement to look for her, gallant as hell, like a knight in shining armor. It's funny to think about now, but at the time, he just wailed and wailed like he was really in love, because there in front of Caleb's magnum opus, he saw Mom suspended, covered in flies, the puzzle's missing piece.

"Bastards, dissidents," Dad blubbered as he uselessly tried to shoo away the flies, but you know how persistent insects can be, they have a thing for decaying bodies. Everyone knows flies have a better sense of smell than humans, and there was the proof: the flies were all over Mom's carcass like a buzzing bacchanalia, a festival of flapping wings, feast enough for all. Mom's flesh would nourish the swarm, Mom was the true altar.

I guess it took a while for the flies to realize how tenacious the man swatting at them was. Slap by slap, they began to withdraw, abandoning the corpse and reluctantly hovering above Mom's and Dad's heads. The more daring ones would land on his hand or her tongue. What perfect places, what grand gardens for the flies.

Dad hollered for us from the basement:

"Caleb! Casandra!"

A moment later, he even called, "Calia!" as if anyone would answer to that name.

Naturally, Calia ignored the sound. She kept munching crayons and sketching a new fly on her blank paper. But that was all, it was just a fly on a sheet of paper, the wings didn't flap, it wasn't alive, it was just a drawing, albeit an anatomically perfect one rendered by a girl genius. Caleb peeked over my shoulder and looked at Calia's drawing, then shrugged and said nothing. Calia isn't the kind of person you ask to explain herself. She won't open her mouth, won't tell us if there was ever a point when the flies were alive or if that was just a figment of our imagination, a mirage born of the lockdown and our yearning for revenge. Caleb just shrugs. He remembers the flies droning their sweet song just as well as I do. He knows those songs have been our only companions during these long days of incarceration. But even the echo of their buzzing has begun to grow dull, just like our sister's bizarre artwork.

Downstairs, in the basement, Dad hollered again:

"Caleb! Casandra!"

We took our time going downstairs. To be honest, we weren't sure what to do. What if this was another one of Dad's tests, designed to confirm out loyalty, or to gauge our response times or retentive capacity? By that point, we never had any idea when we were being tested; the house and the interrogation lab had become very similar places. We were afraid, so we remained in the relative safety of our bedrooms.

"Dad's in the basement," Caleb whispered behind me, pointing down, toward the source of Dad's voice.

His hands were shaking. It's a cliché, but whatever, they were. I guess my brother was worried Dad had discovered his piecemeal masterpiece of torn-up bunny rabbits and kamikaze animals, and he must have been bracing for the reprisal, for everything to come to blows, for Dad to complete his transformation into the director of the interrogation lab who would crush our hands, yank out our fingernails, sic his trained dogs on us, plunge the toilet with our heads, and flush after pissing on our scalps.

"What do we do?" Caleb asked, grimacing.

A heroine to the bitter end, I, of course, replied:

"We go downstairs . . ."

"Seriously?"

"It's two against one, Caleb. If he lays a finger on us, we'll make the sick fuck pay."

"But how . . ."

Okay. So, I've never been in favor of Caleb's bunny-rabbit

sacrifices, and I've never supported his freakish jigsaw puzzle made with the bones of suicidal animals. Mom was right, I'm a monster, just not the kind she was thinking of. Still, at that moment, Caleb and I were what you might call family, or something like it; something that bound the microscopic skeins of our DNA to our survival instinct.

"Do we hit him in the head?" Caleb ventured. "Do we . . . smash his skull in?"

"Uh-huh. I guess. With a hammer. Or a stick. Wait, do you have a stick?"

"No."

"How about a hammer?"

My brother's eyes were going crazy.

"Casandra, come on."

"Look, Bunnykiller Caleb, it's your masterpiece in the basement. You want me to leave you to fend for yourself?"

His silence was reply enough.

"Don't worry, busting someone's head is as easy as smashing a pumpkin . . . I think," I said, immediately feeling nauseous. To be honest, I wasn't crazy about the thought of killing someone, especially not our father, but that's life, adapt or die, and when it comes to improvising based on a given set of circumstance, I'm kind of a superstar.

One of my brother Caleb's few virtues is that he is, in fact, a practical boy. I didn't need telepathy to read his thoughts, which were, like everything in this house, all about the flies: they fluttered above his eyes, his gaze was the ideal score for a symphony of death. You have to admit that, given his kinship with the grim reaper—his status as angel of death and lord of animal suicides—Caleb was well-versed in mortality. His hands abruptly stopped shaking and his lips twisted into a bitter expression that, at another time or place, would have been funny, but not here, not now. He scanned for any sort of weapon, a blunt object, for example, like a hammer or a medieval head-crushing contraption. Wasted effort. I can sum up all his actions with that phrase: *wasted fucking effort*. Our tormentor-father didn't permit dangerous objects in the nation-house, in his utopian family-world. Caleb shrugged and recited something that sounded like a newly learned poem.

"We'll push him hard against the wall, hard enough to crack his skull."

"And I'll take a piece of his brain matter as a tribute to my beloved," I said, joining in the tragical improvisation.

Caleb shrugged, as was his custom.

"Whatever, bridgefucker."

So, we went downstairs. Coconspirators. Barbarians. Adolescent pagans preparing for the sacrifice.

Dad hadn't stopped hollering.

"Caleb! Casandra! . . . Calia!"

There wasn't much light down there, but even so, it was impossible not to see Mom's body swinging in the center of the disarray. She made a beautiful, exquisite corpse. When I say *beautiful*, I don't mean in the obvious, biological sense of the word, because, as happens in all hangings, she had evacuated herself, an unavoidable indignity she must not have anticipated, because she was wearing her dress with the bright floral print. Hers was a cheerful, springtide strangulation. Needless to say, she had on her red stilettos with black soles, the ones that gave her nothing but blisters but which she considered worth it. No beauty without blisters, that had been Mom's mantra, but she would never reflect on the nature of beauty or blisters again, or wonder if she was a good mother again, or think about anything again. Because even if our thoughts and ideas live on after we die, she won't be able to focus on anything except the flies, her new travel companions, who, at just that moment, were crawling over every centimeter of her body from head to toe. Jesus, I'm so melodramatic. I shouldn't exaggerate, sorry. They were crawling over *almost* every centimeter of her body, but here and there you could still see a patch of fabric, the tip of a stiletto, one of her fingers. And of course, beside her stood the great manfly himself, i.e., Dad, who was still bellowing.

"Caleb! Casandra!"

And the instant he saw us or heard our footsteps, he said:

"Help me get your mother down!" and then "We can't let Calia see her! She'll be traumatized!"

When you hate your parents like I do, identifying their character flaws is easy. So now the sick fuck was worried about Calia! About traumatizing her! Ironies aren't always tragic or dramatic, sometimes they're just laughable. I guess the word for that is "tragicomic." So, at that moment, I had to pick up all the shreds of my tattered patience and carefully sew them back together, lest I desecrate the dignity of Mom's demise with my nervous, tragicomic giggle.

I said it once and I'll say it again: being Casandra has never been easy.

Dad turned his back and resumed swatting flies, many of which he swallowed in the process because he kept talking, wouldn't close his mouth, couldn't stop barking orders.

"Get some rags and help! Help me shoo away these fucking flies! Goddamn bugs!"

I looked at Caleb. Honestly, I wasn't asking him to be a psychic, what I was thinking was so obvious that only a shit-for-brains bunnykiller moron like him wouldn't figure it out. Dad had his back to us. He was blind to everything except Mom hang-drying like a sheet covered in flowers and flies. That was our chance. It was all we needed, okay? We even had the element of surprise. Push. Smash. Dad. Dead. But Caleb gave me a look and shrugged.

"We can't just leave her there," he whispered.

My brother. The softy. The bunnykiller. The angel-baby of death . . .

Cacaleb stepped closer to Dad and the flies, and you can guess what happened next, it doesn't take a genius to figure it out, just follow the throughlines of this story and all will be revealed: the flies sensed Caleb's presence and immediately turned suicidal, quit pestering Dad, quit buzzing about Mom's black tongue, and with single-minded focus, sought the angelic herald of death's sanctifying touch.

It happened fast. In an instant, the basement floor was blanketed in dead insects and Mom's corpse, now cleared of flies, hung before us, still swinging and still exquisite, okay? I say exquisite and I mean it because I have very well-founded notions of beauty.

Without a tear, Dad finished lowering Mom's body. The end result? A broken heel. Mom would've hated knowing her best shoes had been so stupidly sacrificed in the clumsy effort to unhook her, but at that moment, no one was thinking about Mom, not even Calia, who was still upstairs drawing to her heart's content, fly after fly, an efficient fly factory meeting all its creative quotas.

I heard Dad's voice.

"The world has lost an excellent mother and an excellent wife," he declaimed, like he was giving a speech, and I'd almost say he wiped a phony, tragicomic tear from his ugly manfly face.

After that, everything was disappointing. I would've loved a lengthy vigil. Our mother's death had to be enough justification to emerge from lockdown, right? And who knows, I did the math and it was possible, between tears and sighs from the mourners and the pseudomourners, I might have had the chance to get away, run eight blocks straight north to the immobile Shakespearean lover who was burning to let me stroke her supports with my skin, desperate to surrender to me in rusty benediction. I'd even decided what I'd wear for the occasion—Mom's black dress, the one Dad said made me look like her—and I'd managed to get Calia to quit chewing crayons for a while, so the three of us could present ourselves as the perfect family in pseudomourning. Even Caleb, after his pathetic stint as human insecticide, had done his part and now appeared to be a regular, sullen, half-orphaned teenager. The expression on his face was almost believable.

"Do you think Dad saw my . . . ?" he asked by my side on the living-room couch.

"Uh-huh, but he must not have cared."

"Really?"

"He would've killed you. Maybe he thought she made it. That'd make sense, right? The way she was acting, Mom could've been the creator of . . . what do you call that thing again?"

"It's a puzzle."

"Right, your puzzle."

Caleb swallowed hard before saying:

"Casandra, I have to confess something."

"I already know—you froze up like a little bitch."

"Talking to you is impossible."

He crossed his arms, started chewing his lip, and gave me the silent treatment in protest. He thought this would make me uncomfortable, but I just sat there fixing the hem of my orphan-princess dress. He was the one who couldn't handle it.

"Did you see her? She was covered in flies."

"They were Calia's flies," I answered, "the flies of the apocalypse or whatever."

"I don't know. Did you see her drawings today?"

"Uh-huh, what about them?"

"*Those* flies weren't alive."

"Yeah, but you also saw the *other* flies, right? The ones before, I know you remember them too."

"I don't know, Casandra. Maybe, but what if we're making it all up?" He shrugged. "I thought they were supposed to be butterflies. Didn't Mom say . . . ?"

"Yeah, I guess there was a miscalculation or something. Either way, they have wings."

"But didn't you see . . . ?" His eyes were on fire.

"See what?"

"Mom was covered in flies. In front of my puzzle . . . she did it for me."

"Did what?"

"Completed my puzzle. Her body was the missing piece."

"Mazel tov," I mumbled with my best ironic tone, which always ends up sounding more ironic than I mean. But hey, what can you do?

"You don't understand," he replied. "You have no idea what the suffering of an artist is like."

"Caleb, you're not an artist, you're a shit-for-brains bunny-killer, and now you're a shit-for-brains flykiller, but unfortunately, you didn't have the balls to become a shit-for-brains fatherkiller. Human insecticide incapable of patricide."

"I mean, if everything goes right, the flies will do it for us, right?"

"I guess. Maybe at some point," I said. Then it was my turn to shrug, and he reciprocated with an almost identical gesture. Sometimes I forget we have the same genes and replicate the same patterns. "Don't copy me. It's rude."

He just shrugged again in response.

That's Caleb for you—a lost cause.

A lost cause who, like me, hoped Mom's vigil and subsequent burial would be an opportunity for escape. It was hard to say what Calia was hoping for, but at least she'd stopped chewing crayons. And she had started drawing more slowly, as if she were exhausted or about to fall asleep. A little fresh air would be good for everyone, and we thought we might get some as soon as that same day, maybe even in just a few hours, after Dad had made the arrangements.

We got dressed. We sat on the living-room couch. For hours. Patiently. Maybe Dad needed time. He was still downstairs, alone with Mom's body.

I'm summing it up quickly but the hours dragged on. Time is a sick fuck.

When Dad finally came upstairs, he didn't even make eye contact.

"Bedrooms, go," was his order.

"We want to say goodbye to Mom," I demanded in my best melodramatic, firstborn half-orphan voice. "It's our right. We want to go to the vigil."

"There won't be a vigil."

"You're gonna let her body rot in the basement?"

Dad's eyes grew wide with horror.

"Cremation."

Thus died our hopes of getting out.

Thus died my dream of being united with my beloved, of melting into her rust as she rusted into me.

Even Caleb was devastated. Maybe he had hoped Tunisia would be at the vigil. Which was a long shot, but at the end of the day, Tunisia was family. Mom had hanged herself, it was a special day, and miracles do sometimes happen. Caleb has dreams too.

"Go," Dad repeated, "now."

We obeyed. Dad's voice was quivering, as it always does before he explodes in rage.

Fear is a sick fuck.

A really sick fuck.

In the house, we no longer heard the resonant click-clack of Mom's footsteps, which we had been using to determine the time of day.

So, I guess this is the big revenge Mom had in mind: leaving us alone with him and the sound of his footsteps, far stealthier than her excoriating heels.

Dad is walking through the hallway.

Now it's just him, us, and the buzzing flies, who are becoming more numerous by the hour. I don't know if they're drawn by Calia or if they're drawn to the fresh cadaver. I don't know where they're coming from, but I know they're here.

Something has changed in the laboratory-house. The girl notices and attempts to eat another crayon, but every time she tries, a hand plucks it from her mouth before she has the chance to chew. The wax comes in different flavors, the reds and blues are her favorites, she gnaws them slowly, and then the red or blue flavor floods her teeth and tongue. Sometimes she spits out chunks of crayon; not every piece is edible, some parts refuse to go down her throat and return to their place of origin, to the tongue cavity, and remain there, fragmentary cud. Calia is angry because the hand continually appears, rummages through her mouth, will not leave her in peace. Why does the hand take away the crayon, why does it steal the crayon, why does it open her jaw and remove her cud? But the hand does not answer her question, the hand does whatever it pleases because it believes that it wears the crown, that it is in charge of the laboratory-house and holds the key to the girl's mouth. How wrong the hand is. How dearly the hand will pay. It is a man hand, the worst kind, plump-fingered.

Today, Calia is not drawing, her papers and crayons have vanished, as has the light of the sun.

All is dark in the laboratory.

Calia has no idea what the word *revenge* means, but something is stirring inside of her, something bright, hot, comfortable, she knows the man hand does not like the wings, does not like the buzzity buzz, she knows the flies are persistent and obey only her, and it is only her whom they do not bother.

Calia's eyes quickly study the sketch, immediately identify where the lines ought to go even through the smudges. The world is one big drawing, one big sheet of blank paper, and Calia spends her days in a state of profound observation. She knows, for example, that the lines of the house are not perfect, they are twisted, disorderly. Chaos is the antithesis of orderly creation. Objects that have abandoned their places of origin are especially noticeable. Calia quickly discovers, for example, a vase in the center of the living room that was never there before. It had always been on the mantle, and in its place on the mantle, there is now an urn that had not previously existed, and if Calia looks even closer, if she pays attention to the sounds of the house, she perceives the click-clack of footsteps coming from the urn, that is, the click-clack of splintered bones, the click-clack of dust. Good thing the urn is sealed; the flies are persistent and eager to get inside. If they had their way, no space in the house would be off-limits to them except for the body of God, the body of Calia. All the rest, truly everything, belongs to the flies, including the urn where Mom's ashes fail at resting in peace.

For Caleb, the worst part of the day is the night, or the time he thinks is night. He has reason to believe it could be some other time. In the outside world it could very well be noon, but that other universe no longer interests the boy. He does not care about anything except the noise, or rather the noises, plural, that Casandra makes. They used to be monotonous, he thinks, but they have grown louder, deeper. In the post-Mom era, Casandra is the only woman in the house, or at least, the only blueprint of a woman to come. Though, judging from the sounds, she will come sooner rather than later. She cries and groans as if a horror-movie monster resides inside her, tearing its way free through her guts. The sounds are not, in fact, a monster, but moans and incoherent babbling, and Caleb is not an idiot; he is aware of what is happening around him, he knows the meaning of that nighttime soundtrack, knows what Casandra is doing, can even deduce what she is doing it with: the camera, or her favorite chair, or some cherished object that has temporarily supplanted her star-crossed lover, because the spirit is willing but the flesh is weak, and maybe iron, cinder blocks, concrete, gravel, and the bridge's mechanical parts are weak too, who knows.

Caleb does not know if Dad hears the same moans that infiltrate his bedroom. It is possible. Dad is not deaf, but he has learned to feign deafness when the circumstances call for it. Adapt or die. Confronting Casandra's cries could cause him to lose face in the family laboratory, which is all that remains of his glorious past. And what is the point of a glorious past without the right to exert influence on your children's hunger, on their bodies, on their will to go outside or not go outside, to draw or not draw, to be or not to be, and he has done well for himself, he has been an eloquent and unyielding dictator who doles out punishment and reward as suits the behavior of the citizenry. A citizenry that, due to recent events, has been reduced to three human residents and a legion of flies. We can assume the human population will remain stable for the foreseeable future, but the fly population is certain to grow. Regardless, uneasy lies the head that wears the crown: Dad will not jeopardize his influence. In every dictatorship, there are insurgents whimpering for revolution, and it does not matter if they produce cries of anguish or ecstasy; both symbolize something cooking in the heat of their fear, or perhaps not quite fear, but a sort of half-baked hopefulness.

For every reaction there is an action, as men like Dad know well. Spasms of any sort, of pain or pleasure, indicate the presence of living beings, and living beings are a dangerous phenomenon that is best avoided. He does everything within his power to make the house a cemetery, an open grave where citizens breathe not oxygen but obedience. Better to ignore Casandra and her disorders. In all human enterprises, there are oversights. Perhaps that is what Dad says to console himself. It is healthy to admit that nothing is perfect, and he has already established that there is bad blood in the family, all it takes is a glance at the children, or at the urn in which Mom and Mom's stilettos returned form the crematory's ovens.

Caleb tries to sleep. In a few hours or a few minutes—he never knows—Dad will get up and conduct his inspection of their bedrooms. There is no telling what he might find in Casandra's. There is no telling if one day he will make her pay for all those orgasms and moans. But for now, Caleb has to sleep, and he tries with all his might to summon what sanity he has left, but Casandra is too loud. She no longer even tries to stifle her cries. If he listened closer, he would hear her skin rubbing against the surface of some object, more than enough detail for his imagination—however limited it might be—to get the best of him, and for his mind to fly to his long-lost cousin Tunisia. There is no telling if Tunisia moans like Casandra, but the image is now firm in Caleb's mind, there is no erasing it.

The sealed-off house is a laboratory, yes, but not the laboratory where Dad concocts his individual power. In this place other ideas are simmering into wicked summer vapors; the house is the older sister's laboratory, Caleb's laboratory, even Calia has her resources. The flies are an extension of the baby sister. The flies have a purpose, and that purpose is torture, torture for all, but for Dad above the rest, their ceaseless buzzity buzz buzz, a vengeful chorus in concert with Casandra's cacophonous climax. Caleb has learned that the house is not just a laboratory, it is a pressure cooker with a faulty valve, and the impending explosion will obliterate everything, including, critically, his dim memory of Tunisia.

Dad's rounds have begun. Room inspection. One by one. He never pulls back the curtains. The sun no longer exists. Dad clears his throat before entering Casandra's bedroom, but she remains unperturbed, she will come hell or high water, she has no intention of relinquishing this orgasm. So Dad stalls outside the door, maybe even hesitates: to knock or not to knock, to enter or not to enter. You never can tell with insurgents, and especially not with insurgent orgasms.

The man believes the dead rest in peace. He does not believe in a life outside the scope of the current one. This belief is important, because, otherwise, if the dead rested uneasily, the man would spend his nights beset by torturous memories—not just of Mom's shoes, but also of the prisoners he encountered long ago and, above all, of these children, his children, whom he is just beginning to understand.

Recollection torments him, yes, but more harrowing are these fucking flies. At first he blamed the rotting, threadbare bones he had found in the basement on the afternoon of the suicide. He razed those remains, destroyed the creation in which skins and splintered bones rested in pieces. He had trusted that the odor would go away and take the flies with it, far from him and his family. After that, he avoided thinking about the altar. He would not allow his suspicions to lead him to the great architect, whoever he or she may be. Better to blame the dead. Better to blame the dead woman and save himself a run-in with the dissidents.

A chubby fly flutters above his head. Tenacious fly. Perhaps it is not a single fly but many, hence the radiant buzzing and droning, damn flies, winged sluts out fucking every night, and laying eggs. There is no negotiating with them; they will broker no détente, entertain no ceasefire. The man with the medals cannot acclimate to their insistence on circling his head, nosediving into his mouth, flying up his nostrils. They are everywhere, there is no escape, and with their slatternly wings, they sully everything they touch.

The morning Calia began speaking was no different from any other. No extraordinary occurrence marked the occasion; there was no before and after. Nothing was out of the ordinary except for the fact that the girl, for the first time in her life, put down her chewed-up crayons, pencils, and pens, left her papers in a corner of the living room, and said:

"God is a big fat fly."

She spoke clearly, without stuttering, without drawing out the syllables, and then she coughed, perhaps choking on her words:

"I do not like beet salad."

And then:

"Beets are not food."

Dad quickly shooed away his own thoughts to concentrate on the voice of the girl who had never before felt the need to speak.

"What?" Dad asked.

"I want cake," she declared, her speech apparently over.

An enormous fly, the chubby behemoth that had seemed determined to infiltrate Dad's mouth, finally succeeded: it entered his open cavity, flew inwards and downwards on a journey from which there was no coming back. Dad had to spit it, half chewed, onto the floor. The creature was still alive, nearly split in two by the man's teeth. It tried to flap its wings or drag itself along the floor, but Dad had an appetite for revenge, and he crushed the fly with his shoe.

"You should not have done that, Father," Calia said. She

shrugged, the same shrug her older siblings performed ad nauseam, an idiotic, half-hearted gesture. "The flies do not like insurgents like you. The Fly God is watching you."

"The fly what . . . ?" He felt the words struggling to come out of his mouth, the telltale sign of a stutter returning to his lips.

"The Fly God sees all rebels," Calia repeated, her voice raspy and worn out; she seemed tired of repeating words that were not immediately understood. "The Fly God says that it is time. The time. Your time. To die."

And with that, the girl returned to her drawings.

Before Caleb and Calia were born, it was just me, Casandra. Not anymore. Now I'm part of an indissoluble trinity. I have been bumped from protagonist to witness. Every morning I sit in the living room and contemplate my sister, Calia, and her works of creation.

The blank page is an ark: everything fits, every sort of existence imaginable. I'm not going to stop to explain what that means step-by-step. Let's just say Calia has an active imagination.

"Casandra," she sometimes says to me, lifting her eyes from the page, "I do not like beets. Get me something to eat. Something that is not beets."

I obey in silence. Now Calia is the one who does the talking, and I've learned to be prudent. Am I scared? I guess. The most prudent thing you can do is close your mouth and open the refrigerator. There's some rotting food in there, but Calia doesn't seem to care if the cake is hard, or the tomatoes are sour, or even if the bread is moldy. She's good with anything except beets. She doesn't complain when she's chewing whatever old food we give her, the leftovers Dad pushed to the back of the fridge, a hodgepodge from the before times.

Chew, chew, gulp.

Chew, chew, gulp.

"Where's Dad?" I ventured to ask her this morning. "What did you do to him?"

"Father is upstairs," she answered with her new voice, a voice I still can't stand. "He is conversing with the Fly God. The Fly God has punished him."

Dad was never a good boy, it's true.

I guess being a good *anything*, a good whatever—like, I don't know, a good man, for example—is pretty hard.

He tried to be a good domestic dictator, that's for sure. Credit where credit is due.

When I go to his room, I don't do it out of pity, I don't do it because I feel bad for the toppled king all alone up there. I go out of curiosity. The curiosity of a child who says he cut open a lizard's belly to see if it really had a beating heart. Justification enough.

The door to his room isn't locked, and it's dark in there, but my eyes adjust.

The human body is super adaptable, and now Dad is trapped in his own interrogation lab, snagged in his own strongman machinery. He's sitting on an old piece of furniture, possibly an armchair, or maybe just on the edge of the bed. Hard to tell in the dark. At first, it looks like he's alone. A pitiful, lonely old man. A sad nobody with bad posture. Then, when I look closer, when my eyes see him better through the darkness, I realize he's in full dress uniform, medals and all.

Then I hear the buzzing.

To be fair, the buzzing was always there. It's part of the background music. That's why it takes me a second to notice. For a long time now, the flies have been part of this family, this laboratory of dictators, great and small.

If the flies obey anyone, it's Calia.

They buzz an ethics entirely their own.

And they're well-versed in vengeance.

There they are, above Dad's body, towering over everything that once belonged to him, laying their eggs, whispering about their housefly hijinks, and shitting all over his medals, his skin, his uniform. Dad is the flies' public toilet. Dad is the Fly God's personal urinal. Dad no longer speaks. He won't utter a syllable. He won't react either.

"Hey," I say as I approach. "Hey, Dad," I repeat, a little louder. "There's no food left downstairs. Should I go get something?"

In fiction, the walking dead would've had a clear reaction. Dad doesn't. Dad isn't even the walking dead; he doesn't even breathe. Even Mom's ashes breathe, downstairs, in the urn, but Dad doesn't.

I go up to him and grab the keys, on which the insects have taken dump after dump.

I close the door behind me. The last thing I see is Dad's silhouette, increasingly covered by the flies, who now form part of his nature, his respiration, his biological processes.

The buzzing isn't going anywhere.

I open the front door for the first time in two months. "No beets," Calia reminds me as I go.

Epilogue

This story's thrilling conclusion is actually super simple, so in the interest of authenticity, I'll refrain from telling it in the style of a Shakespearean tragedy, the way I'd like.

We've never been normal. We weren't normal before the summer and we weren't normal when it was over, when the doors of the house flew open again. The three of us grew up in our own way, as children of the guilty.

We grew up here, in this country, under the tyranny of flies. And I'm all for it, okay? Because the flies have never abandoned us. They buzz above all our dreams and nightmares.

We've gotten used to it. We know the flies aren't going anywhere. And for us, that's good.

Cacasandra.

Cacaleb.

Cacalia.

We reached an understanding with the flies and their tyranny, just like I guess we got used to being Dad's kids and got used to serving as test subjects in a power experiment that lasted the length of that endless summer. Some people have it worse.

I won't say any more about Pop-Pop Mustache. I'll just add that one day he died, as generals and criminals tend to, in an old-man bed, peacefully and in his sleep. He was replaced by another general, this one with no mustache, but with a bushy

Socratic beard that makes him look like a Greek philosopher or an Elizabethan bard.

Dad's fate wasn't so different.

One day he emerged from his room. Stuttering again. The three of us had to get reacclimated to the fecal prefix; it was back for good this time. Money was starting to run low and Dad was worried. He was hungry, but there was nothing in the fridge except frozen pizzas and slices of stale cake, so he went outside, escorted by a few flies who insist on following him wherever he goes; he came back a few hours later, old and tired but with a new job.

We didn't know what the job was for a while.

We didn't know for years.

We were patient.

By the time he decided to tell us, the shame was long gone. He confessed that he had always been fond of animals and the zoo, though he wasn't quite as fond of the smell of their shit after a morning of particularly weighty bowel movements, but who could blame the poor creatures. Their summertime diet was sorely lacking in protein and way too heavy on fruit, and there isn't an animal alive—or a human being, for that matter—who could eat like that and keep its stomach intact. Dad wears a nondescript baseball cap at his job, and he carries around a rake, a broom, and a pail, which he uses to collect shit. The smell and humiliation wore him down at first but, credit where credit is due, our father is a man of his time. A man who has always understood the importance of obeying orders, whether they're given in an interrogation laboratory or a cage full of monkeys in heat. It doesn't matter if he's grilling dissidents or wiping smeared feces from veiny simian butt cracks, Dad doesn't shy away from duty, and Dad doesn't shy away from doody.

He's never told me if anyone recognizes him at the zoo. But they probably do. I'm picturing him inside the primate enclosure, with his nondescript baseball cap, his broom, and his pail, piling a mound of monkey dung like a sandcastle from his youth or his dreams, while on the other side of the enclosure, on the side of freedom, a mother lifts her finger and points something out to her child. Dad will never know if she's pointing at the monkeys in heat or the man in the hat, he'll never find out if that woman is a survivor from his interrogation laboratory—someone who recognizes him and who now, with a simple gesture, identifies him to others—or if she's just a woman like any other, giving her child a lesson in monkey-butt anatomy. That's the worst part: he'll never know, the fear is constant. It doesn't matter that he no longer has medals, because deep down, Dad knows he'll never escape what he did. One day another mother with another kid, or that same mother with that same kid, will march up to the monkey cage and spit a penalty commensurate with the crime.

The flies don't torment Calia, Caleb, or me. Barely at all. The odd buzz. Sometimes they land on our faces, try to wend their way into our orifices. But we have an understanding. We don't swat them away. We live together in peace.

But they are merciless with our father. If Dad opens his mouth, ten flies race inside, land on his wisdom teeth. And Dad lies to himself, which isn't bad, self-deceit can be all right if it brings a little comfort: it's because he smells like shit from the zoo, the flies are just following their noses. But that isn't the truth. The flies have their own identity, an identity with an agenda. They won't settle for buzzing, they are bent on incessant revenge.

Wherever Dad goes, his hands, mouth, and skin are shrouded in a haze of wings.

Sometimes, Dad tells us how much he loves us.

When he does, Caleb just shrugs. Calia doesn't pay attention.

Sometimes, I respond with a half smile, or with a "yeah, Dad, I know," something as nondescript as the baseball cap, part of his new uniform. That's good enough for him.

All of us have an understanding with the flies, but only I persist with my notions of love.

We have a family alliance. When I leave the house, the others pretend not to see. And they pretend not to smell me when I get back, despite the penetrating aroma of rust, which is practically a part of me now. It's my form and structure.

I told you on day one that this was a love story.

The flies get it. That's why they buzz their little love song in my ears, it sounds like a love song to me anyway, the flies never stop singing, not even when I close my eyes.

a note on the translation, potty humor, and capitalist democracy

There's something ostensibly untranslatable in pretty much every book: wordplay, rhyme, cultural references, some especially inscrutable sociopolitical context, whatever. You need to be creative to circumvent these obstacles, but it helps to be non-invasive too. The best interventions are laparoscopic and produce minimal scarring.

In *The Tyranny of Flies*, one of these obstacles is a poop joke. If you've read the book, you know that Dad stutters the first syllable of his children's names, so Casandra, Caleb, and Calia become *Caca*-sandra, *Caca*-leb, and *Caca*-lia. The problem: Spanish speakers say *caca* about as frequently as gringos say *poop*, but in the English thesaurus, it falls pretty low on the list of synonyms for "shit" sorted by popularity (after "whoopsie" but before "meadow muffin"). To make matters worse, in Spanish, "Caleb" and "Casandra" are pronounced *Kah*-leb and *Kah*-sandra, but some English readers may say *Kay*-leb and *Kuh*-sandra, which sullies the novel's scatological humor.

You don't usually translate names. Turning "Raquel" into

"Rachel" is politically problematic, and also just confusing. The fecal prefix caca- doesn't work quite as well in English as it does in Spanish, but it's close enough. The loss is nowhere near significant enough to justify renaming three of this novel's six characters. But if it did, what names could I use? If I were allowed to hack away at this translation with abandon, to create a piecemeal monument like Caleb's dead-animal installation art, what could I come up with?

In one sense, I'm lucky: like caca, two of our most common words for "crap" are a single repeated syllable. I could reverse-engineer the novel so that instead of taking place in an unnamed Caribbean dictatorship that totally isn't Cuba, it takes place in an unnamed European republic that totally isn't France, starring three siblings named Doodoo-Douceline, Doodoo-Dubois, and Doodoo-Doucette.

Or, in a US state that totally isn't Minnesota, starring three brothers named Doodoo-Duane, Doodoo-Duke, and Doodoo-Dougal.

An allegory for the war in Ukraine starring Poopoo-Pooshka, Poopoo-Pootr, and Poopoo-Putin?

Tyranny goes to Bollywood, starring Poopoo-Puja, Poopoo-Purab, and Poopoo-Punika?

There's even a way to retain Hispanic names, if I don't limit myself to solid waste: Could the drama revolve around Peepee-Pia, Peepee-Pio, and Peepee-Pilar?

I've gone through this litany of culturally insensitive poop-and-pee jokes to illustrate that basically everyone, including adults, enjoys immature humor from time to time. I once worked at a middle school where the sixth-graders were fond of using mini whoopie cushions to make fart sounds, which they occasionally supplemented with the real deal. At first, the teachers had a hard time suppressing their own laughter, so for a few minutes before class, they would scour YouTube for its worst, wettest fart compilations to "get it out of their system."

Having spent the past several months channeling the voice of Casandra, I suspect she would have something to say about this hypocrisy. I can almost hear her indignation: *Methinks the teachers doth protest too much, okay? Farting is such sweet sorrow.* But when it comes to shameless double standards, crude humor is just the tip: the long list of hobbies beloved by grown-ups but forbidden to children includes not just fart jokes but swearing, screwing, smoking, shopping, gossiping, gambling, drinking, driving, and dropping acid. Not to mention watching porn or anything else worth watching—while today's grown-ups enjoy the renaissance of great TV writing, we relegate kids to sanitized teeny-bopper dramas and preschool propaganda like *Paw Patrol*. Adults have barred children's access to every vice except TikTok and corn syrup. Of course, like good insurrectionists everywhere, the kids nimbly circumvent our embargos: Casandra still manages to escape for a moment of passion with her bridge; students continue to sneak copies of *Lolita* into Tehran, and copies of *And Tango Makes Three* into Florida.

It doesn't take a literary genius to interpret *The Tyranny of Flies* as an allegory for Communism in Cuba, a metaphorical drone strike against authoritarianism. But as Cristina Morales writes in her foreword, the novel also rebukes the child-hating gerontocracies propped up by "ballot-clasping" adults in the West. I'm half joking when I talk about the double standards above—we probably shouldn't let tweens do LSD—but the regime of restriction, surveillance, and outright violence against kids that *Tyranny* depicts isn't limited to the Caribbean; the "pressure cooker with a faulty valve" where this book's child protagonists live is in our kitchens too. We might have children, we might love children, we might hover over their homework and buzz in their ears like an unswattable swarm of benevolent botflies. But as Casandra puts it, "there's nothing fouler than a father who loves his kids too much." In every sphere of life, grown-up predilections reign supreme; an adult's most trivial whim trumps a child's most basic rights.

Just a few examples among thousands:

During the pandemic, casinos and strip clubs (owned by adults) reopened even as kids were forced to learn pre-calc over Zoom—often unfed or trapped at home with parents (adults) just as abusive as Casandra, Caleb, and Calia's—because nothing's more important than Grandma's slots and Grandpa's boner.

Even before the pandemic, teenage suicide was at an all-time high, thanks at least partially to a set of tools that adults in Northern California created so they could more efficiently monitor and exploit children. But without location services enabled, how will parents (adults) make sure their kids don't take a single unauthorized step? Without social media, how will corporations (adults) monetize every underaged snap, selfie, and sext? Pop-Pop Mustache warns Casandra that in his island autocracy, "the walls have ears"; in our neoliberal democracy, the phones have tracking pixels.

Politicians (adults); lobbyists (adults); and dudes who,

like Dad, have "nothing in [their] head except dreams of retaliation and delusions of grandeur" (adults) insist that every (adult) US citizen must have over-the-counter access to assault weapons, and children get massacred in Red Lake, Blacksburg, Newtown, Parkland, Uvalde, Nashville, et cetera ad nauseum.

As I write, Lockheed Martin and Northrop Grumman (run by adults) are celebrating their best day in years, with stocks up 9 percent and 11 percent despite a dip in the market average, as investors (adults) cash in on those companies' commitment to manufacture thousands of bombs for adults to drop on a 140-square-mile strip of land where five out of every ten human beings is under eighteen. If anyone asks those adults how they sleep at night, they might reply, as Dad does, "I sleep on my side with two pillows under my head and my room and my soul as dark as a dungeon. What have I done besides defend this country's interests at any cost?"

The most obvious violence of all: for the sake of something as ill-defined, as boring and grown-up-sounding as *the economy*— and to meet misopedic adults' demand for cheap flights, plastic everything, and dead-cow sandwiches—executives and shareholders (adults) pump 38 billion metric tons of infanticide into the biosphere every year, auguring in an apocalypse that, unlike the one presaged by Calia's butterflies, isn't fiction.

And, of course, we don't allow our underaged underclass to protest this violence any more than Dad allows Casandra to fuck her beloved bridge. For kids, we close the avenues of justice we otherwise tout as the hallmarks of liberalism: voting, unionizing, striking, suing, lobbying, running for elected office—everything short of domestic terrorism. So, if you want to read *The Tyranny of Flies* as an allegorical drone strike against Communist dictatorships, go for it. But please, save the pressure-cooker bomb for your own Cacapitalist dumbdumbocracy.

Kevin Gerry Dunn
Chicago, October 2023

Here ends Elaine Vilar Madruga's
The Tyranny of Flies.

The first edition of this book was printed
and bound at Lakeside Book Company
in Harrisonburg, Virginia, May 2024.

A NOTE ON THE TYPE

The text of this novel was set in Fournier, a serif typeface released by Monotype Corporation in 1924. It was based on the typeface of the same name created by French typefounder and typographic theoretician Pierre-Simon Fournier around 1742. With its strong contrast between thin and thick strokes and sparse serif bracketing, Fournier was a "transitional" style of typeface, and anticipated the more severe modern fonts that would debut later in the eighteenth century. Its light, clean design presents well on the page, making it a popular choice for printed matter.

HARPERVIA

An imprint dedicated to publishing international voices,
offering readers a chance to encounter other lives and other
points of view via the language of the imagination.